How Amity reacted to the lynch mob at her door would determine the safety of the man she loves.

The welcoming words that Amity had selected flew from her mind when she saw the savage sneer on Ophelia's hate-filled face. . .and realized from the dark clothing that her half-sister was. . .wearing widow's weeds.

"You hussy! You tawdry harlot!" Ophelia cried her rage. "Where is he? Where's the vile Yankee blue-belly you've been sheltering, while his kind have allowed my husband to die in a wretched northern prison and caused our papa to succumb in a hospital after growing septic from his wounds?"

. . . .

"There's no Yankee here," Amity said. . . .

The sisters stood eye to eye, toe to toe. Without any warning, Ophelia slapped Amity with such a force that a crimson stain spread across the younger woman's pale cheek. . . .

"How's come yo' striking my baby?" Mammy angrily demanded as she came thundering down the front veranda steps. . . .

"We're looking to take custody of the Yankee y'all been harborin' here, Mammy," Mister Raynor spoke up. "Y'all best be handing him over."

There was a rope coiled on the horn of the saddle in which he shifted as he waited. Nearby stood a tall tree.

Brenda Bancroft is a pen name of inspirational romance author Susan Feldhake. At home in central Illinois with her husband, Steven, and four children, she is employed as a writing instructor for a college-accredited correspondence school. In her spare time she likes to hike, listen to country and western music, and fellowship with close friends.

Books by Brenda Bancroft

HEARTSONG PRESENTS

HP22—Indy Girl
HP30—A Love Meant to Be

ROMANCE READER—TWO BOOKS IN ONE (Under the pen name Susan Feldhake)

RR7—For Love Alone & Love's Sweet Promise

Don't miss out on any of our super romances. Write to us at the following address for information on our newest releases and club information.

Heartsong Presents Reader's Service
P.O. Box 719
Uhrichsville, OH 44683

When Comes the Dawn

Brenda Bancroft

Heartsong Presents

ISBN 1-55748-407-4

WHEN COMES THE DAWN

PRINTED IN THE U.S.A.

one

May 1864
Atlanta, Georgia

Heat and humidity made the late afternoon air cling to the skin like wet wool. Amity Sheffield's cheeks were red from the warmth, and her wavy blond hair curled in tight wisps that accentuated her oval face with its pert dimples near her small, neat mouth.

"Hurry and change your frock, Amity! The gentlemen callers will be arriving before we know it. We must be ready," the older, severely dressed woman said in a stern voice.

The slim, pretty belle halted and glanced over her shoulder, sighing, a look of supplication on her weary features.

"Oh please, not tonight, Ophy! I can't bear it," the seventeen-year-old girl protested. "I'm tired, and besides, I have plans of my own. There are things I want to do. Laboring for the cause as we all are, there simply aren't enough hours in the day to get accomplished what we desire."

Amity looked away and so escaped seeing Ophelia's reaction. Her half-sister pursed her lips, and her brows forked over indignant eyes.

"And what plans, pray tell, are more important than graciously entertaining the troops of the glorious Confederacy? What can possibly take precedence over giving our brave young men a moment's respite so that they can return to the front lines and gallantly fight the blue-belly Yankees with honor and hope, protecting the way of life that we cherish and hold dear?"

Ophelia's tone brooked no argument and convinced Amity that it was futile to try to reason with her. The young belle swallowed her feelings.

She wasn't about to admit to a staunchly Confederate woman like Ophelia that her plans centered on a promise given to Serena, one of their household slaves. Amity had been helping Serena with her reading and writing each day after the Sheffield slave finished her many tasks.

Amity instinctively knew that Ophelia wouldn't approve of educating a servant. Her recently married half-sister often decried the plight of the South since the Yankees had begun rabble-rousing, encouraging dissent, and inspiring once loyal household servants and field hands to abandon the townspeople and plantation owners who had provided for them.

Amity couldn't risk incurring Ophy's wrath. It had been pointed out to her time and again that Ophy had been invested with sole authority when their papa had galloped off to war. Amity knew that Ophy took perverse delight in thwarting her younger sister's desires.

Ophy wouldn't cotton to the news that Amity had located a tattered primer from her own early schooling and was teaching their servant to read. But Serena had a quick mind and a love for knowledge. With an eye to being able to read the Good Book for herself, Serena had the motivation to stick with the task and seek random moments for study throughout her task-filled day.

Amity gave a resigned sigh. Ophelia had certain expectations as well as specific ideas of what was proper behavior. Teaching household slaves how to read and write wasn't a task with which she'd feel her younger sister should concern herself, nor a pastime that she could condone by looking the other way.

For days now, under the guise of Serena helping Amity tend to her hair and draw her bath, the two girls had closeted themselves in Amity's rooms. They kept their voices hushed, their heads close together, as they focused on the page. By the flickering light of an oil lamp, Amity helped Serena sound out the letters to form words.

Amity couldn't help grinning with delight when she saw the triumphant smiles that tugged at Serena's lips when she succeeded in haltingly reading line after line. The night before, after Serena had finished reading a section from the primer, Amity had read a chapter from the Bible.

"Time for us to get to bed," Amity had said when she had finished reading.

"Yes, Miss Amity. Ah reckons it is. We's got de washin' to do in de mornin'. Not only that for de fambly, but some for de folkses at de hospital, too."

"Then this had better be all for tonight. We can read again tomorrow night. I promise. You're doing so well, Serena. Soon you won't need help at all."

Serena's eyes had sparkled in the light of such praise, and her face had grown soft with dreamy reflections.

"I cain't hardly wait 'til I can read the Bible," the young slave had said, beaming. "Leastways, someday I hope to be able to. 'Til then Ah'l be prayin' that some kind soul will let me hold their precious Scripture between my hands, so's I can read the words of our dear Lord m'self. Mayhap you will?"

"Maybe someday," Amity had said, giving a quick smile, "you'll have your very own Bible to look at any time you have the desire."

Amity knew that there were unread Bibles tucked

away here and there in the Sheffield household, and she had made a mental note that when Serena's birthday neared, she would try to locate one to give to the servant without Ophelia's knowledge.

Generally, slaves' birthdays came and went, unnoticed by the people they served. Amity sensed that Ophelia wouldn't approve of her presenting a slave with a gift, even one of small value. Well, what Ophy didn't know wouldn't hurt her!

Amity sometimes wished that not only could she give Serena a Bible, but that she could give the girl her freedom as well. As quick a student as Serena had proven to be, and as friendly and sweet as she was to be around, a sudden bond had sprung between the girls of such differing stations in life. Serena had always been so thoughtful and helpful that it now gave Amity a pleasant feeling to consider the way Serena would treasure a book that the Sheffield family owned but apparently hadn't had any desire to read.

While Serena had made wonderful progress during their weeks of clandestine study, Amity knew that she herself was receiving the most valuable education. She had a new appreciation for the knowledge that she had always taken for granted. Seeing the miracles possible in the arrangement of letters in the alphabet through Serena's appreciative gaze had

opened Amity's eyes to the injustices between owners and slaves throughout the South.

"The young gentlemen will be arriving at any
time," Ophelia said, jerking Amity from her thoughts
with another sharp reminder. Ophelia crooked
her neck, casting a sharp glance down at her
bosom where an elaborate golden brooch-watch
was securely fastened. "See to it that you are
present on the front veranda in time to welcome
them."

Amity sighed wearily, helpless not to let her pique
show. She dragged a tired hand upward to rake her
heavy hair away from her face and off her shoulders.

"Ophy, I'm so tired I can hardly put one foot ahead
of the other. Those wash baskets of linens were so
heavy. I was worn out by the time I arrived, and then
Serena and I faced the long walk home from the
hospital."

Ophy gave a piffling wave of her hand.

"And isn't it a pity that Milady Sheffield had to
walk to the hospital because a gallant beau couldn't
come callin' in a dashing hack to ease the burden of
duties that obviously you are unable to perform
without complaint!"

"I'm not complaining. I'm glad to do my part. But
I'm exhausted, Ophy. Tired!"

"I don't care if you are tired!" Ophelia snapped, her

hazel eyes flashing as her temper flared. "Have Mammy tighten your stays to fit your best frock. Brush your hair. Bring a smile to your lips and a sparkle to your eyes.

"Then get out on the veranda so you'll be there when our gallant Southern soldiers come to call. I shan't have them marching on down the street to dally with other belles on the block because there's no one with a ready welcome at the Sheffield residence."

Ophelia paused long enough in her litany of commands to narrow her eyes, and their hazel color turned greener as jealousy overtook the plain girl's features.

The envy that Amity believed she saw did not become Ophelia, and for a moment Amity was struck by how unappealing the bossy young woman really was. How Ophelia had managed to appeal to the man who had married her was more than Amity could imagine.

"Your poor, poor husband," Amity sighed under her breath, not caring if Ophelia heard or reacted.

But that thought was overshadowed by the uncharitable idea that her older sister was so insistent about Amity making a timely appearance on the front veranda every night because the soldiers expressed more affection and admiration toward Amity than toward herself. At least with Amity present, Ophelia was offered reflected attentions, and the gentlemen favored her with courtly, gallant conversation.

Then there was the possibility that Ophy's competitive nature motivated her to want to constantly triumph over their neighbors. While Ophy seemed to dislike Amity as a person, she did approve of her younger sister's looks, if only because they prompted the soldiers to call at the Sheffield home rather than at the Brewster girls' home farther down the street.

It was little social contraventions like that which mattered in Ophelia's eyes, and mattered more than Amity believed was necessary. Sometimes Amity felt pity when she detected such fear, insecurity, and desperation in Ophelia's myopic stare.

Recently there had been an air of utter seriousness in Ophy's earnestness about Amity being on the veranda. No evenings was she excused from the activity. A thought washed into Amity's mind and made her feel as if she'd been caught in a cold wave. Perhaps with their father off to war and Ophy invested with power, she saw it as her duty to marry off her young sister before tongues could start wagging and Amity could be labeled a pitiful spinster.

Amity could almost hear the way people would whisper behind their fans. They would start to genteelly and oh-so-worriedly wonder whatever was wrong with Miss Amity—so pretty on the outside, but perhaps so inwardly flawed that no gentleman had seen fit to claim her for his bride.

Well, she had had her chances. The truth was that she'd had no desire to wed. While the beaus she'd spent time with had been handsome and attentive, none had ever made her heart beat fast nor filled her daydreams with affectionate notions. She'd never entertained the sensations that had made some of her girlfriends become giddy, giggly, and in Amity's view, silly.

"*Let* the soldiers visit elsewhere," Amity said in a testy tone, "if that's what they prefer."

"But they *don't* prefer those simpering silly girls to ladies like us," Ophelia assured. "How could they?"

Amity gave an unladylike shrug.

"Perhaps they do," she said, yawning. "Did you ever stop to ponder the idea that they might stop here to do us a favor by passing time with us rather than have us spend a lonely evening?" Amity patently enjoyed watching her sister's complexion grow mottled and florid in reaction to her question.

"Balderdash!" Ophelia snorted in a display of worried ill-temper. "Now, whatever your prior plans, postpone them and do as you are told. Papa would be very dismayed if he knew how defiant you have become since he placed you in my care. When he returns home from the battlefield a hero, I shan't spare a word in telling him exactly how recalcitrant you've been!"

At the thought of her father off to war, his life in danger, Amity was drawn back to the present moment's needs. That grave specter drew her away from her desire to assert what independence she could muster in the face of Ophelia's bullying.

"And furthermore, young lady," Ophy said in a snippy tone, "you can make up your mind to be charming instead of wallowing in your usual mulish attitude!" Ophelia withdrew a lace-decorated linen handkerchief from the basque of her best frock and mopped at her face, suddenly dripping with perspiration.

"You should be thankful that you can do your part for the cause," she added, "by reminding our brave boys in gray of the genteel belles and courageous womenfolk they're fighting and dying to protect! It's the least you—we—can do."

Ophelia took a deep breath and archly patted her wilted, frizzing hair into place. "I fully intend to entertain the brave gents on this fine summer's eve— just as I hope some other woman is giving *my* dear, brave, patriotic husband a moment's respite from the war."

Amity grimaced. Perhaps that was it! Was Ophelia desperate for Amity to marry so that she could shed the responsibility of caring for her young half-sister? The way Ophy carried on, the appearance of Union General Grant or the dreaded William Tecumseh Sherman wouldn't dissuade her from insisting that Amity take up her position on the porch.

It was as if Ophelia were manning the trenches in a desperate battle to rout soldiers from their competitors' front porches and victoriously capture their presence on the sheltering Sheffield veranda shielded by towering sweet gum, sycamore, and magnolia trees.

Amity physically weakened over the thought of the evening's activities. Further arguments would only tax her reserves. She admitted defeat.

"Very well, Ophelia. But could I please postpone my appearance for a little while? After all, I spent all morning in the backyard with Mammy and Serena stirring boiling kettles full of putrid bandages.

"My afternoon was spent pinning cleaned bandages on the clothesline, taking them off when they had dried, and then folding them with Serena and loading them in baskets we bore halfway across town to the hospital. That is, when I wasn't being forced to stand still while Mammy dabbed buttermilk on my skin to keep me from freckling in the sunlight.

"Haven't I done *enough* rushing around for one day? Can't I at least take my time freshening up and dressing?"

Ophy's back stiffened, and a flash of hatred sizzled through her eyes. Amity suddenly became aware of the depth of resentment the older girl experienced whenever her authority was challenged.

"Don't be such a selfish goose! I labor, too, but do I complain?" Ophelia asked in an imperious tone. "One would think that you would be flattered that young men come to call. Those cross-eyed, weak-minded Brewster girls can't get the gentlemen to visit them, not even during these troubled, war-torn times. No doubt they'll live and die piteous old maids, the focus of everyone's scorn.

"So consider yourself fortunate that you are receiving social calls and are enjoying the attentions of prospective young men from good Southern families. Those girls would give anything to get a swain to cast so much as a glance in their direction."

Silence spiraled between the two. Ophelia was waiting for Amity to defy her, and the younger girl found it impossible not to respond.

"They're nice girls, at least," Amity muttered. "Far easier to get along with than some people I know."

Ophelia gave Amity a haughty glare.

"You're an insufferable piece of baggage, you are," she hissed, and her eyes widened with outright malice.

At that moment, Amity knew that Ophy would love nothing better than to be freed of any obligation to her sister. Marrying Amity off would remove the burden of the solemnly sworn commitment she'd given their aging father.

When Amity made no retort, Ophelia spoke on.

"Such mulish behavior! Did they teach you nothing at the Academy for Young Ladies? If you don't learn to conceal your unseemly attitudes," Ophy added in a dour tone, "you'll live and die an old maid.

"Most of your friends are already married; I work with them at the hospital. Believe me, they are talking about you. What they are saying isn't flattering, either.

"And," Ophelia hesitated in her tirade long enough for another attempt at taming her tangled, strawberry blond tresses, "I shan't be surprised if your prior reputation didn't harm my chances of making a good matrimonial match earlier than I did. The young gentlemen considered us as alike as two peas in a pod until my dear, insightful husband took a closer look. He liked what he saw and realized that I am nothing like you."

"Why, thank you," Amity purred, giving a serene, unruffled smile that caused her dimples to merrily come into play. "I do declare, Ophelia, that's the sweetest compliment I've heard all day."

Mammy walked through the hallway and gave a rotund chuckle.

"Ah 'spects that ain't been no problem fo' de young gemp'mums, Miss Ophelia. Yo' two young misses be as diff'rent as day an' night! Sho' nuff ain't no worry 'bout *dat* consideration!" She lowered her voice so that only Amity would hear her. "She best be hopin' her young gemp'mum don' take an even closer look. He might be tempted to step a-fore a Yankee bullet!"

Amity smiled as Mammy winked.

"I didn't catch what you said, Mammy, but it's clear that you're aiding and abetting my recalcitrant sister. Therefore, you'll hush your mouth—or risk the consequences," Ophelia said in an angry hiss. "Continue on as you have been, Mammy, and perhaps I shall dispose of you as Pa should have done decades ago."

Before Mammy could react, Amity did. She crossed the room, her eyes narrowed. Drawing up to her full height, the outraged girl faced Ophelia.

"You hush *your* mouth," Amity spoke, her tone

flaring hotly as it trembled with anger. "You know the esteem in which Pa holds Mammy! He put her in full charge of the household when he rode off to join the troops and fight for the cause. He only invested you with the power of the elder white woman of the household."

Ophelia gave an unconcerned sniff.

"Mammy may think she's in charge of the household, but I am in authority over the persons in it. See how much authority she would enjoy if I didn't give it to her. Now, this is an order: freshen up and join me on the veranda, Amity. At once."

two

Stoically resigned to the night ahead of her, Amity set about bathing and fixing her toilette. Twenty minutes later as she arranged her hair in a becoming style, she studied her reflection and realized that the bloom of womanhood was upon her youthful features.

It was there for young gentlemen who were considering settling down with a wife and family to notice, even though Amity had tried to ignore the feminine changes herself.

She was well aware that most of her childhood friends were married, just as Ophelia had pointed out, and some of them held babes of their own. A few girls who had married young had toddlers at their knees.

An alarming number of them were aged beyond their years, and more than a few were already wearing black. Scarcely had their brave Southern soldiers made them wives, than the hated Yankees had made them widows.

While their positions as wives of the Confederacy

had given the belles certain social freedoms, it had also presented exhausting burdens for them to take up in service to the glorious cause. Matrons, who were no longer viewed as innocents needing protection, were not excused from the gruesome tasks that it was deemed unseemly and indelicate for belles to perform.

The matrons were expected to do the worst tasks at the hospital, shrinking from nothing lest they be accused of shirking. Married women and widows were expected to aid in surgery, nurse the infected, delirious soldiers, and touch the dead.

Amity was a practical girl with a thirst for knowledge. She had an innate ability to apply logic to situations in what Ophelia frequently accused was a most unladylike manner. Amity knew she would earn the scorn of eligible beaus who didn't wish to be challenged by a mere woman.

After spending no small amount of time thinking it over, Amity could see no benefit to marriage. Rather, her logic led her to see many drawbacks, not the least of which was that she had not met a gentleman who stirred within her any sense that he might be the man meant for her: the one who could make her heart quicken, who could fill her with warm feelings by a mere look, a tender smile.

In times gone by, sometimes at cotillions, barbecues, and family reunions, Amity's friends had talked in giggly tones and blushed with indescribable emotions that they shared like members of a secret society of those who were loved and were in love.

But Amity was not one of them. Because she was a pretty girl, Amity had always had plenty of beaus. Not one had ever caused her to feel the emotions that she knew her girlfriends had suffered when they had met the men of their dreams. She had never felt that united with any beau—certainly not to the point of being unable to imagine life without him. She had never met a young man with whom she could imagine herself growing old, content to love only him.

Amity wasn't going to settle as easily in love as Ophy had. Once Ophelia had focused on Schuyler, the poor fellow hadn't stood a chance. Ophy had seemed desperate that he might get away before he said, "I do."

Fortunately, with her appealing looks, Amity believed that when she chose to marry, she wouldn't have to marry for anything less than true love.

Amity touched the powder puff to her nose. She ached with tiredness and felt anything but charming and vivacious. Even the application of scented talc failed to liven her spirits.

The young girl dreaded the evening ahead. Sometimes Ophy could be embarrassingly transparent in her efforts to marry off her younger sister. Amity hoped it wouldn't be another evening of humiliation featuring Ophy presenting her as a shopworn item to be disposed of to the first person willing to take possession.

Love and marriage weren't supposed to be like that. Amity couldn't imagine marrying a man for whom she felt no more than she did for the men she regularly encountered. She knew from the descriptions of her closest girlfriends that she had not once entertained the feverish passions of the heart they had enjoyed when they had become betrothed.

Amity corrected herself. She had not known what such feelings were like until that very afternoon. She closed her eyes and relived the thrilling, heartwarming experience.

Hours earlier, as the searing sun had begun to travel a western path, Amity and Serena had struggled with the willow laundry baskets brimming with freshly laundered and folded bandages.

Straining to catch their breath, the two women, a respected young belle and her house servant, had made their way into the massive brick building pressed into service as a hospital.

Surrounded by the hubbub—crowded bodies on pallets, humming conversations, and screams from the surgical quarters—the two women, one white and one black, had gazed around the cavernous room, intent on catching the eye of a staid matron so that they might release the bandages into her care.

Amity had been searching for a familiar face when she had seen him. Him! The man of her dreams.

Serena had been unaware of the transformation her mistress was undergoing. For her part Amity had felt as if she had been suspended in time. It had seemed as if that very moment had been ordained from the world's beginning.

The handsome soldier, as if guided by a power far greater than the both of them, had looked up. Amity's heartbeat had quickened, wondering if there would be a special element of recognition. Although they were total strangers, she had felt that they had always in some special way known each other.

The soldier's expression had at first been fathomless, but a moment later he had regarded her with a touch of curiosity, if only due to the boldness of such a pretty belle's stare.

Amity's lips had curved into a hesitant, trembling smile. She had fervently wished that she were wearing her most becoming gown. To her relief, the soldier had given her an acknowledging smile. His frank gaze had never left Amity's eyes, and she had been incapable of breaking his capturing glance.

"Yo' all right, Miss Amity?" Serena had asked,

concerned that her mistress had frozen in her tracks. She gave the young belle a worried, scrutinizing look.

Amity had tried to reclaim her poise.

"Yes—yes, of course. Just feeling a bit faint," she had added in a breathless tone.

"Yo' sure?" Serena's concerned frown had deepened. "Yo' seems to be takin' on a might bit strange, iffen yo' pardon my sayin' so, Miss Amity."

"Don't worry, Serena. I won't swoon," she had promised, but a moment later she had feared that she might, such was the intensity of the man's gaze. His eyes—blue eyes that she could drown in—had been riveted on her.

"See that yo' don', Miss Amity. Ah expects dey's gots 'nuff to do here 'thout yo' causin' them concern." Serena had wrinkled her nose at the malodorous scents that attracted buzzing flies and increased the suffering of the sick and dying men.

"How the matrons an' widder-women stands to serve the cause myst'fies me. Ah 'spects dey's consolin' theyselves they's allowin' the Lord to use 'em as He will to give comfort to dey fellow mans."

"I expect so," Amity had echoed agreeably, her mind wandering off as her eyes had remained riveted upon the soldier who had turned back to his labors of mercy. Amity had been left feeling bereft, robbed of something precious.

"Oh, there's Miz Crispin!" Serena had cried with hearty relief.

Without waiting for her mistress, she had plowed ahead with the brimming basket, calling out to the stout, stern-faced matron, whose demeanor made it clear that she tolerated no lallygagging nor tomfoolery.

In Serena's sturdy wake, Amity had stumbled along, struggling with her own basket. She had not been concentrating on where she was going. Repeatedly she had looked over her shoulder for one more glimpse of the handsome man who had somehow touched her heart, a handsome soldier of the Confederacy who was destined to disappear from her life, never to be forgotten.

"We's got fresh bandages, Miz Crispin, Ma'am," Serena had said softly to the weary woman wearing a blood-stained gown and gore-splattered apron.

Beulah Crispin had distractedly taken custody of the baskets. She had positioned her considerable bulk so that she shielded Amity from catching sight of an indecent display in the surgical rooms.

Then with brusque, dismissive movements and a quick word of thanks, she had shooed Amity out, pointedly gesturing toward the front doors and the street that was teeming with Confederate soldiers who were milling around, waiting.

The recent influx of troops had swelled the city's population beyond the customary twenty thousand inhabitants. Johnny Rebs seemed everywhere now that the Yankee devil, William Tecumseh Sherman, had forced his way into Georgia, commandeering the railroads to do so.

It was rumored that Sherman was intent on placing a stranglehold around the city and bringing Atlanta, and the South, to its knees. Southerners didn't doubt Sherman's plans, for he had forged steadily onward, destroying everything in his path as he neared his destination: Atlanta, the heart of the Confederacy.

Recent nights while seated on the veranda fanning herself, sipping lemonade or sweetened fruit juices, Amity had heard men argue and discuss battle strategy until sometimes her thoughts swirled from the onslaught.

In the darkening moments of those evenings, she had wished only that people could live in peace. But she kept her own counsel, never daring to breathe a word that she much preferred her servants' companionship and conversation to her sister's. Such sentiments falling from the lips of a genteel Southern woman would have appalled everyone present.

That afternoon, as Beulah Crispin had showed her to the door, Amity had glanced in the direction of the tall, dark-eyed, ebony-haired Rebel soldier. Desperate for the opportunity to exchange another smile with the stranger, she had sought an excuse to stay in the building, if only for a few moments.

"Perhaps Serena should run along home," Amity had suggested, her voice casual. "I could remain and help, leaving when Miss Ophelia departs for the day. Miz Crispin, y'all seem terribly busy today. I could pass out water, fan away flies, read to the men, write a letter home to a loved one, or—"

Beulah Crispin had given a tired smile and patted Amity's arm gently, as if she wasn't fooled. Even among the rigors of war, the dour matron could recall what it was like to feel one's heart stir for the first time. But duty was duty, and decency must be maintained.

"We *are* busy, child," she had acknowledged in a gentle tone. "Another trainload of wounded arrived in Atlanta an hour ago on the Western and Atlantic line. They were spillin' off the trains and bein' unloaded off litters before the surgeons had dispatched with all the sick and wounded who had come here last night.

"But you run along and leave now," the matron continued. "These are not scenes to be taken in by innocent eyes. 'Tis getting bad enough that I'll be dismissing Miss Ophelia to go home within the hour.

She's got several years on your age, but even so, she's innocent compared to those of us who are mothers and grandmothers, and if 'tis in my power, she will remain thus. So be off with you, girl!"

Amity had known that there was no room for further discussion. As a brash and chattering Serena had led the way to the street, Amity had glanced back, hoping for one last look. The Johnny Reb who had so suddenly captured her heart was gone from sight. Amity had been awed by the void that his absence created within her.

But it didn't make sense, she had told herself. It was silly. Surely such feelings as she had entertained weren't returned by the handsome soldier. It was just a girlish whim. It was more likely that laboring beneath the noonday sun and standing over a wash kettle in the suffocating heat had made her feel giddy and susceptible to odd and unacceptable ideas.

On the walk back to the brick house where she had lived with Mammy, Serena, and Ophelia since her father had galloped off to the front in a rush of political fervor, Amity had hardly noticed their surroundings. Her thoughts were filled with vivid impressions of the handsome Rebel whose likeness would always remain within her heart.

When she had realized that she didn't even know his name, Amity had experienced an acute sense of loss. The sensation had refused to go away, even when she had reminded herself that there was no such thing as love at first sight. That it would be futile—and foolish—to daydream about a hauntingly handsome Johnny Reb she would never see again.

The girl was yanked from her musings by Mammy, who finished lacing Amity's stays by giving a solidly crisp tug. Dusk draped over Atlanta and footsteps could be heard progressing up the city sidewalks, as soldiers strolled beneath the boughs of sheltering trees.

"There, Miss Amity," Mammy said. "That's done."

"Thank you, Mammy." Amity turned away, hesitating, making careful movements as she adjusted to the added pressures exerted by the whalebone corset.

"Which gown yo' goin' to wear this evenin', Miss Amity? Dey's all clean an' pressed."

"Her best frock." From across the upstairs bedroom came Ophelia's flat-toned, irritating answer.

"I'm quite capable of speaking for myself and of deciding which dress I'll wear!" Amity flared. Then, even though she knew her best frock was the most becoming, she selected a less elaborate gown.

"This one, Mammy," she said, retrieving the gown from a hook as she cast her bossy sister an impudent look.

"No, Mammy. I specified exactly which frock Miss Amity was to wear. Replace the one in your hand with the garment on the hook," Ophelia instructed.

"I don't give a tat what you said, Ophelia Sheffield! If Pa were here—" A furious Amity sputtered with resentment as her eyes flashed like heat lightning across a summer sky.

"It's not Sheffield any more, my dear," Ophelia trilled in a proud tone. "It's Emerson. Mrs. Schuyler Emerson. Or did you forget?"

"How could I?" Amity retorted. "You won't let me—or anyone else—put from mind that your husband is a major in the Confederate Army. Is that why you are suddenly issuing so many commands? Did he entitle you with military power as well as give you his name?"

"Don't be petty, Amity. It's not becoming," Ophelia ordered.

"If Major Schuyler Emerson is as awful to his troops as you are to the members of this household, his men must feel like throwing in their lot with the blue-bellies or shooting him in the back and considering the glorious cause well served!"

Ophelia's cheeks became red splotches and her eyes narrowed. She whirled to face her sister, and her slashing eyebrows met over glaring, yellow-green eyes.

"Breathe another word like *that* within my hearing, Amity Sheffield, and I'll have Mammy make your mouth foam with lye soap!"

"Why, you—"

Amity's lips clamped shut against the furious words that sputtered in her mind as once more Ophelia's behavior brought out the worst in her. She feared that if the confrontation continued, she would be squalling like a scalded cat, and the soldiers in the streets would be able to overhear an unladylike debacle.

Mammy's kindly pat on her bare shoulder encouraged Amity to act like the proper lady that beloved Mammy—who had raised the girls when pneumonia had taken Amity's mother, and Ophelia's stepmother, eight years earlier—had seen to it that she was.

"There, there, Angel. Don' you pay her no mind. It don' matter what she thinks of y'all. Not when yo' know that you're doin' an' behavin' in ways to give yo' own heart content."

"Mammy, why can't she—won't she—just leave me alone?" Tears filled Amity's eyes. Her beseeching whisper rose to a miserable wail after Ophelia swept out of the bedroom and down the stairs to oversee efforts in the kitchen where Serena was preparing dainty refreshments to be offered to what troops would come calling that evening.

"I don' know, Lambie. Maybe because Miss Ophelia wants yo' to fin' a gemp'mum, marry, an' be as happy as she is."

"Happy?" Amity gave a weary laugh. "How can she be happy—unless she finds joy in making others miserable? In persecuting those unfortunate enough to be around her?"

As Mammy helped her dress, Amity poured out a deluge of words describing the horrors of the war in a low-pitched litany of hardships, denial, disappointment, and despair.

If only she could spend the evening with her head close to Serena's curls, their eyes riveted on the velvety pages of a primer worn soft from the use of many students learning how to read.

Amity knew that Serena would be disappointed, and she vowed that she would make it up to the slave girl. She would find a private moment to whisper to Serena that they would steal away to read at a later date.

"These be tryin' times, Miss Amity. You're right, darlin'. But what all you jus' said 'bout de war. Well, that makes Miss Ophelia right, too. The brave gemp'mums needs to be able to slip away from the hospital, them that's well 'nuff to walk, and go callin' on Atlanta's pretty belles. That way they can forget 'bout the misery 'til the trains take 'em back to de front lines again."

"I suppose you're right."

"And who knows?" Mammy said, tossing Amity a wink as she gave her a comforting hug. "Maybe one of these gemp'mums will touch your heart the way Mister Schuyler did Miss Ophelia's, or. . . ."

As Mammy droned on with reason and encouragement, Amity felt increasingly morose. It had been a lifetime since she had known balls, barbecues, hunts, cotillions, and grand parties.

The young men she had known then, who she had believed had been destined to become her beaus, had been dressed in foppish fashions. They had come to call astride the finest saddle horses in the South.

With swaggering good health, dashing looks, and doting, wealthy families to indulge their whims and back their bravado, they had joined the Confederate Army, looking stunning in exquisitely styled gray worsted uniforms of the finest quality fabric.

There were times when Amity doubted that there was a man left whole to be found in the entire Confederacy. Girls who a few years before would have turned away from impoverished, disfigured beaus were wedding them in droves. They were marrying while they had the chance—before eligible men could be returned to the front lines and the girls would find themselves forever pitied as spinsters.

The once debonair boys in gray were now clothed in ragged garments of butternut brown homespun. Their health and wealth had been stripped. Still they gallantly came courting—minus an eye, missing an arm, limping on a peg, supported by a crude crutch— possessed with the air of redolent swains who knew that they only temporarily endured hardship and viewed it as a minor inconvenience.

These boys believed that victory was as close as the next battle, but Amity couldn't take such a belief to heart when many situations within the South contradicted what, deep down, she knew was right.

"Yo' pretty as you can be," Mammy pronounced as she set the hairbrush down on the marble-topped dresser and adjusted the tortoise shell comb holding back Amity's honey blond hair that fell in swirling waves around her shoulders, accentuating the creaminess of her skin. A locket drew attention to the frilly, ornate bodice of her gown.

Mammy winked at Amity, crossed the room on quiet feet, snatched the cut glass decanter containing Miss Ophelia's lavender toilet water, and dabbed the cool, expensive scent to her favorite's skin.

"Amity!" Ophelia called up the stairwell. "There are young men arriving on our neighbors' verandas. Your presence is required!"

"She'll be right there, Miss Ophelia," Mammy assured. She gave Amity a consoling pat.

"You jus' ignore her, Miss Amity," she suggested in a kindly whisper. "I knows yo' tired, so jus' think about your dear papa out there fightin' the blue-bellies, an' yo' content yourself that yo's entertainin' each young gemp'mum as iffen yo' were having the Good Lord come to call. Consider how grateful yo'd be for a chance to lighten our Savior's cares. Then yo' can more graciously do the same for some others. An' do it with a glad heart."

"Yes'm, Mammy," Amity agreed, sighing, although the kindly woman's faith-inspired words were lost upon her. Faith was something the slaves concerned themselves with, but Amity had never found the time for such issues. Nor the need.

three

Just as Ophelia had announced, tattered Confederate soldiers were proceeding up the streets. Although their clothes would have been discarded by them at one time, deemed unfit to serve as rags to rub down a lathered horse, their courtly manners remained endearingly intact.

A few beaus whom Amity had been acquainted with before the war, she now viewed with pitying alarm. Once they had been well-fed, glowing with good health, immaculately groomed. Now they were aged beyond their years, their frames emaciated from hard work, lack of sleep, and poor diets.

Too many meals were made of doughy paste of flour, cornmeal, water, and a bit of salt formed into ropes and wrapped around ramrods. The dough-covered ramrods were extended over open campfires and baked until hard. The resulting hard biscuits filled the soldiers' bellies but did not nourish their spirits, and accomplished little else for their bodies.

The southern boys had been able to endure such

deprivation for a short while, but as the battles had dragged on, and supplies had grown more scarce, their physical stamina had been depleted, leaving them prey to sickness and other complications.

Banter was lighthearted even during times of war, as if the soldiers recalled their upbringing and managed to find the wherewithal to assume the role of gallant swains come to call.

But instead of a band playing background music at a cotillion or ball, there was the muffled report of cannons in the distance. So accustomed were the men to the cannons' boom, the crack of rifles, and the report of black powder pistols that they seemed immune to the noise that Amity still found disconcerting.

She marveled that the nearing battles somehow seemed remote from them as they relaxed on the veranda and entertained themselves with harmless gossip and the news of the day.

After a decent interval that allowed the men time in which to feel at home, Mammy and Serena quietly circulated among them, graciously serving delectable refreshments.

Without making comment, seeming functional and undemanding as pieces of furniture, the household servants threaded their way among the clusters of soldiers gathered at the home that Morgan Sheffield had recently departed, going north to join forces with the men attempting to block the Union Army's progress into Georgia.

Recently talk had been of little else.

Ol' Jo Johnston and his troops were dug in up in the mountains, forming a stronghold. Johnston vowed to stand strong forever, but he needed men to do so, and he begged for troops. Begged to little avail.

The Confederate forces were outnumbered two to one, and morale was low. The soldiers were in dire shape. Their feet were bare, their bellies were empty, and they knew that their kinfolk at home were suffering just as terribly.

Desertion had become a real problem. There were those who simply walked away from the battlefield with no intention of returning. They were footsore and heart weary, tired of fighting. Then there were those who had left, but only temporarily, and without bothering to get permission. They were taking "plough furloughs" to go home and help their folks on the plantations.

Who was going to plant the crops with the darkies running away? How were their families going to support themselves with no crops in the fields? How would their kin subsist when the Confederacy's own commissary department was as ruthless as the Yankees?

Citizens of the South felt that the commissary officers were as deplorable as the Yankees. What the hated blue-bellies didn't steal, the Confederacy's commissary officers commandeered.

And so the numbers of men fighting for the South dwindled.

Patriotism moved some of the soldiers to request transfers from their units. There were soldiers who were serving with the commissary forces, mail units, hospital staffs, and those assigned to maintain the railroads. Some of them began to request transfers that they might be sent to the side of Ol' Jo Johnston who desperately needed them.

In recent weeks the Yankee scourge, Sherman and his forces, had worked to rout Major General Joseph E. Dalton from the rugged terrain in northern Georgia, unmapped territory with underbrush so thick that the Rebs and Yanks could pass within a few feet of each other, unable to see the enemy that they could hear nearby.

There was fierce fighting. Sherman knew better than to try to dislodge Ol' Jo and his men, for it would require bloody hand-to-hand combat. So he sought to cause Ol' Jo and his men to give up their position. He began to swing out, arcing wide of the area, planning to sweep around the Rebel stronghold and reach the railroad.

Ol' Jo, realizing the Yankee officer's intent, ordered his men to fall back and then fight. It became a pattern. Fight. Fall back. Fight some more. Retreat. Battle again. Always the Rebels remained with their backs to the railroad.

The Confederates had seen what the Yankees had done in the past to destroy their transportation systems in an attempt to cripple the South. When a rail line was captured, droves of blue-bellies set upon the gleaming tracks. They ripped up the steel rails, rooted out the ties, then stacked the timbers in huge mounds. They slanted the heavy rails over the windrows of wood and then set the piles ablaze.

When the heat from the ties turned the rails red-hot, the Yankees, with sweat pouring from their skin due to the intense heat, used timber to bend the rails so that they would be unusable. In the South, where supplies were precious and replacements were difficult or impossible to acquire, such destruction left the railroad unsalvageable.

Amity had heard more than she cared to know about how the battles were being fought not many miles to the north. There were times when she let her mind drift to more pleasant thoughts in order to escape the reality of her existence. Some of the callers at the Sheffield residence, seeming to sense the young woman's boredom with details of the battle, sought to introduce more pleasant topics.

Most nights soldiers who came calling either spoke of their families back home, discussed kinfolk or friends held in common, or mentioned prominent political acquaintances so that conversations were more like those they had enjoyed before the war.

But on that evening, talk was only of war. Almost everyone still had faith in Ol' Joe Johnston, the respected Confederate officer in his midfifties. He had taught the accursed Yankees a lesson at Chickamauga, and any day now, they contented themselves, he would teach the blue-bellies another that they wouldn't soon forget. They had confidence in him. Ol' Joe wouldn't let them down. There was no way that he would allow Atlanta, the storehouse of the Confederate States of America, to be overrun by Yankees.

Atlanta, with her foundries, produced cannons, rifles, train rails, armor plating, and warehouses to store goods that provisioned the whole South. Atlanta—the city that provided huge hospitals to preserve life within the wounded—also manufactured wooden coffins to contain the remains of the dear and glorious dead who had given their lives for the Confederacy.

The pride and faith the soldiers had in Ol' Joe was matched only by the contempt and hatred they had for the Union General William Tecumseh Sherman.

Although it galled the soldiers to admit it, the dreaded Yankee commanding officer knew the northern Georgia terrain as well as Ol' Joe, and he wasn't about to be tricked into a trap that would make his men fight in close quarters.

"Don't worry," one of the soldiers assured everyone gathered on the veranda. "General Johnston can stand forever at Dalton."

Silence spiraled up.

"I don' know," another Johnny Reb murmured worriedly. "We're in trouble if they can't hold 'er. I've heard talk that maybe Jeff Davis is thinking of replacing Ol' Jo with Lieutenant General Hood."

There was some quiet dissent, then one voice rang out above the others, firm with assurance.

"Jus' rumors. Maybe a threat. He won't do it, though. Not if Ol' Jo can stand strong," the first soldier stressed. "And he will, especially if they'll send him the troops he's crying for."

There was a murmur of voices, creating a dull roar of conversation. Each man had an opinion on that score.

"Y'all know Gov'nor Brown's refusing to release his militia?"

"Well Ol' Jo wouldn't be beggin' for Governor Brown's Pets if he wasn't in dire need. Maybe he's gettin' too old to command. Mayhap we do need a feller like Hood to step in. He's a young fellow— only thirty-three—and wild as a bay mule. Full o' spit and vinegar. Perhaps that's what's called for. An officer with some spark an' fire to impassion and inspire the troops as he leads 'em into battle!"

An older man with a heavily bandaged leg thoughtfully puffed on his pipe and dolefully shook his head.

"He's impulsive, that Hood. When I was a young pup, I used to be a tad on the impulsive side, too." He drew on his pipe. "An' I learned quick enough what it got me."

"That's right," the fellow next to him agreed. "Too rash, if you asked me. He came within four demerits of bein' kicked out of West Point, y'know. That says somethin' about his character and his capacity to lead when a cool head an' calm manner may be required to sort out the various options."

There was a gabble of disagreement from across the porch.

"Regardless, you can't discount his bravery. Hood's left arm was shattered at Gettysburg. An' he lost a leg at Chickamauga a year ago. But does he sit in a rockin' chair and let action pass him by while he fills his mind with past glories? No sir! They have to strap him into the saddle so he can lead his men—but lead 'em he does!"

"Well, iffen he's goin' to lead troops, they'll have to be sendin' them to him in numbers sufficient for him to do what must be done."

"I'll be there soon as I get the word," a young man vowed.

"Me, too."

"I'm with y'all!"

"We'd be in good company among each other. When we go back to the front, who'd want to do battle alongside troops like Gov'nor Brown's Pets anyway? Too pampered to face the war and fight like other Confederate men."

"Don't y'all worry. Jus' remember Chickamauga a year ago!"

They did, and in discussing that rousing victory, faith and hope for immediate triumphs sprang anew, even though there were wary mentions of recent skirmishes at places where Rebs had strongholds, where Union forces had bivouacked too close to home: Rocky Face Ridge, Crow Valley, Ringgold, Dug Gap, Snake Creek Gap, Dalton, Reseca.

As the velvety warm night cloaked Atlanta and katydids scratched in the darkness, Amity hid one yawn and then another behind the fan she wafted to create a breeze in the stultifying heat. The soldiers continued to discuss C.S.A. strategy.

In the glow of the coal oil lantern that Mammy had

hung on a newel post bracing the veranda's room, Amity made out approaching figures. She looked up, and her lips parted in surprise. *He* was there. Dazed, she stared, sure that it was an apparition created by her exhaustion and the daydreams that had crowded her fanciful thoughts.

But when she blinked, the handsome Rebel soldier who had so completely captured her thoughts had not disappeared, and Amity gasped in wonder as he strode up the steps to the veranda, a pace behind Will Conner, a young gentleman Amity had met long before at a ball held near Grandpapa Witherspoon's plantation not far from Jonesboro. As an old family friend, Will was accorded a position of respect and welcome above and beyond the formal welcome offered to the pleasant strangers who congregated on the Sheffield porch.

Amity hardly heard Will as he presented himself, saying sweet, courtly, complimentary things to her. Due to her rigid training at the Academy, she murmured instinctive greetings and managed to afford Will a quick smile before her eyes were drawn to the handsome stranger.

At close quarters she savored his perfection. Surrounded by the South's men, the tall, dark-haired stranger was the only one who wasn't relying on crutches, or dealing with cumbersome bandages, or obviously recovering from near fatal infection or disease.

Even so, a fresh pink scar created a thin line at his temple, disappearing into his hairline and signifying a grazing wound that, but for a miracle, would have been an instantly fatal injury. Around his upper arm was a bandage, soiled, but otherwise dry, offering evidence that it was a minor injury and he would soon be returned to the front. Perhaps he would not be so fortunate during a second encounter with the dreaded Yankees.

At the realization, Amity's heart skipped a beat then flew to a staccato rhythm as she fleetingly considered the unfairness: just when she had met a potential beau who stirred feelings in her from the first glance, it was clear that he was destined to depart without a chance to woo her, if that was his intent.

Amity suddenly understood what her friends had experienced. And she knew why they had agreed to almost indecently quick weddings in order to have time to spend with the men they loved.

"My new friend saw you at the hospital today, and he let me know that he would like to make your acquaintance," Will Conner drawled, gesturing toward the silent stranger who gave Amity a reserved smile and ducked his head forward in humble greeting.

"Yes. I. . .I noticed him," Amity breathed, returning his smile while trying not to appear too forward.

"His name's Jeb Dennison, Miss Amity," Will said. "And Jeb, I present the loveliest belle in all the South, Miss Amity Sheffield of Atlanta, the fair city's most charmin' female o' courtin' age."

Jeb took Amity's hand in his. The contact was as special as she had known it would be, and when she looked into Jeb's eyes, she was aware that he sensed something out of the ordinary, too.

"How you do run on, Will Conner," Amity accused, but gave him a pleased smile as she waited for Jeb to say something—anything—to which she could respond personally.

When Jeb did not say a word, the quicksilver thought flitted through Amity's mind that he was shy, although the looks they had already exchanged had certainly been bold enough.

Before Amity could plumb the significance of Jeb's silence, Will matter-of-factly offered an explanation for his friend's stoicism.

"He's a mute. Jeb can hear whatever y'all say to him, Miss Amity." Will touched his own throat. "But he cain't answer. An paper an' a pen ain't always easy enough to come by. He wrote me a note that he was injured during a fracas with Sherman up north aways, knocked out by a blow to the head, and left for dead in the underbrush. Drifting in and out of consciousness he finally woke up on the train bearin' him to the hospital.

"Jeb can't talk, so it's been difficult for him makin' his way an' gettin' the point across to folks about what he's doing and what he needs. He's been spendin' his days helpin' with the wounded who're worse off than he as he finishes recoverin' himself. There would probably be a few more families readin' casualty lists and grieving for their dead if not for the miracles this Johnny Reb's worked." He gave the taller man a warm look and continued his explanation.

"I expect that his pappy was a physician, for he seems t' know more than just a little about the healing arts. But if you want to communicate with him, y'all will have to phrase things so he can answer by shakin' his head yes or no. It makes it a bit easier an' less laborious than expectin' him to write out his responses."

"Very well," Amity said, managing to keep a tight rein on her emotions so that her face and tone did not give away her keen disappointment.

For long minutes Amity's smile was frozen to her features. Her heart felt as if it had shattered. She couldn't bear for those around to witness her private heartbreak, nor could she stand the thought that Jeb would know her torment in discovering him less than the perfect suitor to fulfill her every girlish dream.

As time passed, Amity felt more in control, and gallant as Jeb was, it somehow became easier to forget that he was hampered in ways that other men were not. Jeb was, by far, the most handsome man on the veranda, and Amity knew that he was also the most attentive.

His doting eyes seemed to convey more than all the other young men's bantering conversation could begin to contain. He gave her looks that spoke to her soul, and she sensed that the glances she sent his way addressed him in a similar manner.

Gradually, as streams of soldiers began to pass by en route to their army quarters or the hospital, those who had come to wile away the evening with Amity and Ophelia prepared to depart and came forward to tender courteous goodbyes and thanks for the tasty repast served by the Sheffield slaves.

When it became time for Will's leave-taking, Jeb moved forward, too. Jeb presented himself first to Ophelia, then to Amity. He took her hand, lowered his lips to it, and smiled. His eyes conveyed the intimate messages that his lips could not speak.

When their gazes met, Amity saw Jeb's desperate look and recognized the anguish of one denied something desperately desired. She realized that never before had she so much wanted to hear a man's words, and never so keenly had Jebediah Dennison desired the power to speak to a woman.

"Do come calling on us again, Mister Jeb," Amity invited. "And you, too, Will," she added, if only out of gratitude that he had brought the man of her dreams into her life once and could be counted on to arrange it again.

"Mightn't be none of us back," Will idly warned as the pair left. "We may be subjected to cannon thunder in mere days." He leaned against a brace post, and stared off into the dark distance, as if he saw a dark future.

Amity's heart squeezed in dismay as Will tendered a quick goodbye and with a courteous nod, Jeb took his leave and followed after his friend.

With Will's last comment, the talk shifted back to the war. Those who remained seemed unable to restrain themselves from discussing the fearful future.

Ophelia Emerson began receiving quiet advice from the older soldiers who granted her a certain stature as the family decision maker. She had been put in a position they wouldn't desire for any woman, but which necessity had forced many southern women to accept.

"Y'all really should think about leavin' Atlanta while you can, Miss Ophelia," a man, the father of three, who now walked with a crutch, urged the young woman.

Another man quickly agreed. Soon it was the unanimous sentiment among the men who remained on the veranda.

"You've no doubt seen that folks have been leavin' in droves. You should go while you can. Some say there's not a need—and pray God that it won't become a necessity—but the fact is that while you may resist the idea of fleeing, you can travel now in relative safety south on the Mason and Western, and east on the Georgia Railroad.

"When the time comes that you want to leave— *have* to leave—that may no longer be true. Sherman took over Union railroads. Our own Confederacy may be called to do the same. Civilians will suffer in order that the C.S.A. may be served."

Ophelia's fingers flew to her throat. Her pale face grew more wan.

"But—but they have promised that Atlanta won't fall," she protested. Her mouth opened and closed, but for a moment no sound came out. "They say it can't fall. My husband, Major Emerson, has assured me that they will never allow Atlanta to come under siege."

The men nodded, but their faces were reluctantly grim.

"An' like as not it won't, Miss Ophelia. But it could be unpleasant living here, and y'all might see things unfittin' for womenfolk to witness if we're forced to drive the blue-bellies from these very streets, one man at a time."

That suggestion brought a gasp from Ophelia as she looked around, seeming to imagine Yankees swarming over every stoop and hiding behind each shrub, while cannons were booming, howitzers shrieking, and rifles cracking.

Shaken, she began to stutter frightened, disorganized pleas. Her eyes sought assurances from the soldiers that things were not as grim as these veterans of many battles had seemed to suggest.

"There's no denyin' that the battle lines are falling back, Miss Ophy. We'd be lyin' to you if we told ya different. The truth of the matter is that the Yankees are pressin' closer every day, ma'am. The Yanks can't be but much more than thirty miles t' the north. Time's running out."

"Oh my," Ophelia whimpered, looking-around, her eyes darting in panic. "What'll happen to us?"

"We're hopin' that Ol' Jo will stand strong. But there ain't no guarantees in life. Atlanta is the jewel of the South. Stands to reason that the Yanks are going to work hard to capture Atlanta. The onliest way I can see for them to accomplish it is to choke off the city. To lay it under siege."

"Siege?"

"Yes'm. I'm afraid it could come to that. Prayin', mind you, that it won't. But realistically facing that it could."

"Oh my," Ophelia whimpered. "Siege. . . ."

As she said the dreaded word, the soldiers began to talk in hushed, grim tones of what this could mean. Food on short rations at first, then running out as starvation set in. There would be no newspaper, for there would be no paper supplies, nor ink with which to print.

Yankee forces would cut the telegraph wires to prevent news from getting into the city—or getting out. There would be no mail service, and no rail schedules would be maintained. In such a closed and chaotic environment, rumor could run wild, with mob action close on its heels.

"Y'all have kinfolk out in the countryside, don't ya?" A kindly, gentle-toned man inquired, seeming to take control of the situation with his question. "You should leave Atlanta before the threat of siege grows stronger. Once it arrives, there won't be no leavin'. Then it could be too late. Have you a safe place to go to wait out the war and bloodshed?"

Ophelia looked stricken. Her trembling fingers crept to her throat and nervously toyed with a locket.

"Well, yes, there's Major Emerson's kinfolk. And we've got our Grandpapa Witherspoon, too."

The man ducked his head in a gesture of respect.

"Then I'd suggest that you, your sister, Mammy, an' your cook go visit kinfolk 'til we've sent those heathen Yankees packin' and dispelled the very specter of a siege."

Ophelia wrung the linen hanky in her damp hands.

"We'll think about it," she promised.

"I ain't meanin' no disrespect, Miss Ophelia, but y'all best be doin' more than merely givin' it consideration, ma'am. Y'all had better be following through on the suggestion."

"How soon?"

The man leaned on his crutch and rubbed his bearded jaw.

"Well, if some bloke was givin' my woman and her kin this advice," he seemed to carefully choose his words, "I'd be hoping he'd give the same answer I am: Tomorrow mornin', ma'am. Jus' as soon as y'all can make arrangements to leave Atlanta. Go. An' Godspeed."

"Tomorrow," Ophelia suddenly agreed in a dazed tone. "Very well. We'll depart in the morning."

Stunned, Amity stared as if she were sightless

while the soldiers took their leave until all that remained was their boots echoing against the hard sidewalk as they disappeared into the distance.

After issuing crisp words to Mammy and Serena to pack the trunks before they took to their cots for the night so that they might be able to leave as soon as Ophelia could find passage for them, Major Schuyler Emerson's wife swept into the house and up to her quarters. Amity remained alone in the darkness. Her eyes were dry, but her heart was awash with unshed tears as she realized she would never see Jeb Dennison again.

four

The next hours passed in a nightmarish blur. There were clothes to pack, household items to store away, and furniture to cover. It was well past midnight before Amity was free to slip on a nightdress and lie down on the feather tick. She was almost swooning with exhaustion.

Alone in her bed, plagued by heady feelings each time she remembered the touch of Jeb's lips to her hand, Amity understood what had driven her friends to the altar in haste. She didn't know how she could face the dawn knowing that soon Jeb would be but a faint and fleeting memory.

Amity felt as if she'd scarcely fallen asleep when Mammy tiptoed into the girl's sweltering upstairs bedroom and shook her awake. Ophelia had already left for the railroad depot to arrange their passage and to find someone to haul their trunks to the train station.

After Amity dressed, she drifted downstairs to eat a solitary breakfast. Mammy and Serena, occupied with last minute chores, seemed relieved that Ophelia had left. From the quietly hurt remarks the servants exchanged, Amity realized that Ophelia had been inordinately sharp-tongued and short-tempered with the loyal Sheffield household help.

Mammy and Serena worked quickly and in uncustomary silence, conveying to Amity that they were as upset by the radical change as she. Amity sensed that they were as frightened by the unknown that lay ahead as she was.

It was midmorning before a heat-wilted, visibly nettled Ophelia returned home, waving her flower-bedecked straw hat since she had no fan with which to move the sultry air about her.

"That's done," she said, and wearily reiterated what extraordinary lengths she had gone to and what trials she had faced to arrange passage for the four of them on a Macon and Western railroad train departing from Atlanta later that day.

Fanning herself and passing smelling salts under her nose, Ophelia sank into a chair and sent Serena scurrying for a cup of tea with which she would revive herself for the journey ahead.

"We depart for the plantation of Schuy's family in two hours," she reported. "I've telegraphed them that we will be arriving some time late this afternoon so they will be there to meet the train. I know it's not much warning, but that can't be helped. We're family to them now. They can't—and won't—refuse us hospitality."

Ophelia's words held more conviction than the expression on her face. A chill gripped Amity's heart when she considered what lay in store for them if they were not welcomed with traditional Southern hospitality.

Mammy, Serena, and Amity exchanged concerned glances. But from the scowl on Ophelia's features, they knew that she would brook no comment nor endure any questions regarding the matter.

Although no one had spoken a word, they had assumed that they would be going to Grandpapa Witherspoon's plantation where Amity's mother had been raised. Mammy had lived there until she had come to Atlanta with her young charge who had married Mister Sheffield, a widower. They had become part of the Sheffield home which included Mister Sheffield's motherless little girl, Miss Ophelia.

The three people placed in Ophelia's care had not expected to be guests at the Emerson plantation, even though it had been an option raised by Ophelia to the soldiers the evening before. Logic had dictated that they'd go to Grandpa Witherspoon's plantation. Amity had never given a thought to the idea that Ophy would select Schuy's family to host them. If she had, she would have registered a complaint the evening before.

Mammy and Serena exchanged unhappy glances, but said nothing. Amity, however, was unable to contain her feelings for a moment longer.

"Oh, Ophy, you didn't!" she cried, upset.

Ophelia gave her young sister a cool stare and patted her heat-dampened, frizzing hair into place as she took the cup of tea from Serena without a glance of thanks.

"Why, I most certainly did. And I will not tolerate your taking on so, my dear. I'll have you know that I am long overdue a visit with my new kinfolk at Magnolia Manor. It's my home now, too, you know.

And, it so happens that Schuy's got a cousin," Ophelia added with a knowing smile. "He's home from the front lines for good because he's wounded a bit too seriously to be expected to fight any more, and well, he might be interested in *you*, Amity. Papa Emerson mentioned him in a recent letter as a likely and worthy prospect. You could do worse. And it's high time you found a husband, settled down, and. . . ."

Amity felt weak with horror. For a moment she stared, stunned.

"What?" Amity whispered. "What did you say?"

After the daydreams about Jeb that she'd had the day before and the sweet musings before dawn, to think of another man as a possible husband seemed an emotional infidelity. For others to have the power to strike a matrimonial bargain involving her filled Amity with horror.

"With Pa away, I have to think of such things—especially since you fail to consider your future." Ophelia blithely defended in an airy tone. She twitched her long skirts into place and nestled the teacup on her prim lap.

"Cousin Philomen would be a steady man. You could do worse. There's not much to choose from these days, I might remind you. And, my dear, you are getting older."

Only Mammy's gentle hand on Amity's forearm restrained her from uttering hot, hostile words that would have had Ophelia ordering Mammy to fetch the lye soap.

"I spoke with Hettie Adams on the way home," Ophelia announced. "Jubal and Absalom will haul our trunk and valises to the railway depot. They should be arriving at any moment."

She glanced at the timepiece brooch pinned to her dress, an heirloom that had belonged to Schuy's late mother.

"We don't have any time to waste, so I hope that you're all prepared to depart with no lallygagging nor shilly-shallying. From all I've been told, the railroads aren't terribly reliable these days. What was once a short trip now might very well take all day."

The household was a hive of activity as the four women attended to last minute tasks. When everything was ready, Ophelia locked up the residence and hurried down the street.

The two servants and Amity followed in Ophelia's wake as she rushed Jubal and Ab through Atlanta's streets. Time and again she craned around and in a testy voice bid her retinue to hurry lest they miss the overcrowded train.

All too soon, they arrived at the train station. The sun beat down, and Mammy and Serena stood in stoic silence on the weather-beaten, splintery railroad platform. They didn't dare express their fears about life at the Emerson plantation where they'd be expected to take orders from Schuyler's kin, the Emerson servants, and their own young misses.

To Ophelia's chagrin and the misery of those who were forced to be around her, the train was more than two hours late. While they waited, the travelers dared not leave their place in line for fear that they would be unable to find places on the train when it arrived.

They were hot, thirsty, and almost fainting from the searing sunlight when the belching locomotive arrived, a plume of dark smoke drifting up into the cloudless sky as it chugged toward them. With a grating clash of steel against steel, the train drew to a stop in front of the depot.

Slowly the line inched ahead as people labored up into the aged and dusty railroad cars, gingerly seating themselves on the once plush upholstery that was now threadbare, offering mute testimony to the general decline of the Confederacy.

By the time the locomotive chugged away from the depot, Ophelia's tinder-short temper had grown even flintier. She snapped at everyone she confronted, but she couldn't help offering a smug, self-satisfied smile at those who were forced to wait beneath the relentless summer sun for the next train.

"I so dread accompanying Ophelia to her new kinfolk and so detest the idea of socializing with Misses Lavinia and Maybelle Emerson and making the acquaintance of Cousin Philomen, that I would sooner remain in Atlanta and run the risk of having blue-bellies coming to call," Amity muttered to Serena. "I don't know how we will stand it."

Mammy gave an unamused chuckle.

"Maybe we be runnin' into dem Yankee gemp'mums anyways," she dared to venture an opinion. "Mist' Witherspoon's plantation is more remote. Pro'bly would've been a heap safer there than at this here Magnolia Manor."

"I doubt that safety counted for so much as a tat when Ophelia made our plans," Amity sighed.

"We're in the Lord's protection," Serena reminded. "Nothin' will happen but what He allows it."

"That's right, girl," Mammy agreed. "We cain't be a-forgettin' that. If the Lord be with us, cain't nothing win against us—leastways, not in the end."

Amity had no such solutions, herself, and she envied how calmly the slaves faced the journey to a distant area and a strange household. As the slaves quietly chatted back and forth, mentioning names Amity suspected were from the Bible, she realized that they knew stories that she did not.

She listened to Mammy and Serena remind themselves of men and women who had pleased the Lord, men and women who had faced the risk of leaving behind what they had known and wandering into a strange region because it was the Lord's will.

Let the slaves dream, Amity thought. Maybe they thought the Lord was leading them south of Atlanta and that by obeying they were doing His will, but Amity knew better. Ophelia was in full control, and she loved every moment of making decisions that could change the destiny of other people.

The locomotive roared over the countryside, seeming to chew its way through the pine forests and mowing down the hillside. But it struggled up the grade, huffing and puffing, moving more slowly as it lost momentum. Passengers seemed to strain ahead, as if shifting their body weight could help the train to crest the hill.

A groan shuddered through the passengers when the locomotive fell short of power just before the top of the hill and the train coasted back down. The engineer had no choice but to put the locomotive into reverse and chug backward, almost pushing the caboose up the hill they had just descended.

Men heaved more fuel into the fire boxes. The blaze ignited. The water roiled. A blast from the steam engine's whistle was proof of increased pressure.

The engineer let the pressure build a bit longer, then he eased out on the throttle. Faster and faster the locomotive went, chugging determinedly. It slowed, but enough of a run had been taken to provide the necessary momentum. A hearty cheer overtook the car as it conquered the hillside.

The train continued to make progress, but precious time was repeatedly lost when the engine failed to crest a hill on the first attempt.

Ophelia was simmering when, in sight of their destination, the engineer pulled onto a siding to let a train bearing weary, sickly men in blue uniforms pass.

"Yankee prisoners," someone said. "They be takin' 'em down to Andersonville."

Amity shuddered. She knew that Andersonville was the dreaded prison camp. She tried not to look into the cars that inched by, but she couldn't avoid seeing the prisoners. A few Yankees' eyes met hers, and she gave them sad half-smiles in sympathy of what lay ahead of them.

When at last the prison train had passed, the train from Atlanta pulled out from its siding and drew into the station. The Emerson girls and their pa were waiting at the depot when their weary callers from Atlanta arrived.

Raynor Emerson led his guests to a dilapidated carriage that was hitched to a mule. His horses had been commandeered by Confederate forces, a sacrifice the kindly gentleman claimed he had been glad to make. Amity wondered about this because she knew from remarks that Schuyler had made that his father's horses had been his pride and joy.

Mister Raynor was the same courtly gentleman Amity had remembered from Ophelia and Schuyler's wedding, but as the evening wore on, she realized that she liked Misses Lavinia and Maybelle even less than she had recalled. It was clear that they remained silly girls, both simpering and vain.

At Magnolia Manor, Ophelia, who considered herself a true Emerson, was in her element. Amity, Mammy, and Serena were steeped in misery, feeling like sojourners in a foreign land.

Never had Amity felt like she was such a burden, and the unpleasant emotion escalated when coy announcements were made that Lavinia and Maybelle both had intendeds and would be wed within the fortnight when their beaus came home on furlough from the front lines where they fought for the C.S.A.

Almost on the heels of that announcement came the news that Cousin Philomen would be stopping by to welcome the visiting kin from Atlanta.

"Miss Amity's looking forward to making his acquaintance," a calculating Ophelia assured, causing Amity to quail inwardly. "In fact, Miss Amity, in Cousin Philomen's honor, I think that you should go to your quarters and pretty yourself up a bit."

Ordinarily Amity would have protested, but any excuse was suitable if it removed her from the Emerson girls' presence.

"Take Serena along to help you," Ophelia ordered.

The shy-eyed slave quickly fell in step behind her mistress.

"Are you going to marry him if they want you to?" Serena whispered when they closed the doors to Amity's room.

The slim, pretty blond whirled, her eyes blazing.

"When donkeys fly!" she hissed.

"Maybe he's nice. Philomen, that's a name from the Bible," Serena said. Then she sounded it out.

"You really miss your reading and writing, don't you, Serena?" Amity asked.

The household servant gave a hesitant nod.

"Yes, Miss Amity, I do."

"We'll continue with it," Amity promised. "Even if we have to sneak to do it."

"I've seen some books that are available. Maybe if

you'd ask, Miss Amity, they wouldn't mind your borrowing the Good Book. We could read it in your room."

"I was thinking more in terms of dreadful penny novels myself," Amity said. "They have some tremendously good love stories."

"The Good Book got some love stories, too," Serena said. Then she began to describe some of the stories she had been told, but had never known the joy of reading for herself. "Mayhap you'd like readin' them to me, iffen I couldn't read them to m'self right directly."

"Maybe I would," Amity said, intrigued by the idea that the Bible could have some love stories between men and women of God, written centuries before.

The two girls dawdled in Amity's room for as long as they dared before they rejoined the Emersons. Amity felt as if she had been given a reprieve when the heavily promoted Cousin Philomen failed to appear that night. She was as relieved as the matchmaking Emersons seemed disappointed.

By the time she could offer excuses and escape to the guest room assigned to her, Amity had a grinding headache. She stared out over the darkened meadows, and the sight only made her feel worse. The cotton fields were covered with weeds and brambles now that poor times were upon them all.

Silently Mammy slipped in bearing a ewer and basin containing soothingly hot water for Amity's bath. The thoughtful servant had brought linens and soap from Atlanta. Without a word, she began undoing the closures of Amity's clothes, helping her from her garments as she had when Amity had been a sleepy little girl.

"I don't think I can stand it here, Mammy," Amity murmured in a tremulous whisper. "Lavinia and Maybelle are silly and petty. It exhausts me listening to their prattle. And around them, Ophelia is even more domineering and derisive than usual. The way they are carrying on about him, Cousin Philomen is sure to be repulsive."

Mammy didn't offer a word of disagreement.

Amity clenched her hands into fists.

"I can't marry him!"

"Especially when Serena and I's knowin' you're so taken with that young soldier who came callin' last night." Mammy paused reflectively. "My, my, seems like a lifetime ago, not jus' yesterday, Lambie."

Amity met Mammy's eyes in the beveled mirror.

"You noticed?"

Mammy gave a rich laugh.

"Of course I did. And so did Serena. That mute boy couldn' take his eyes off you either. Maybe he can't utter a word—but his eyes said it all. Compared to him, you'll sho' nuff find Mist' Philomen wantin'."

"I know I'm going to hate it here. I already do," Amity whispered in a bitter tone.

"Maybe it'll be better in the morning," Mammy suggested, but the remark lacked any conviction.

"Well, if it's not, I'm. . .I'm not going to stay. That's all there is to it."

"You've—we've—got nowhere else to go, honey. Yo' heard the menfolks talkin' las' night, and again when we got off the train in Jonesboro. You've listened to what Mister Raynor said at the supper table. They's expectin' Atlanta to fall. Y'all can't go home. We ain't gots a home to go to 'ceptin' this one—and the heavenly mansion waitin' fo' all o' God's chillun when He be callin' 'em home one day."

"But I can go to Grandpapa Witherspoon's home. And I will, Mammy, I promise you that. I will even if I have to walk every step of the way."

Mammy set the basin aside. Her face took on a nostalgic cast.

"Now that's a fine man, Mister Witherspoon. Why, I remember when your mama was a lil' girl, we were all so happy there. It's still like home to me."

"You'd like to go back, wouldn't you, Mammy?"

The bulky, aging woman gave a rotund laugh.

"Heavens, yes, child, I reckon I would."

"Do you know the way?" Amity whispered.

Mammy's eyes grew large as she stared at her

young mistress and plumbed the possibilities the headstrong girl might have in mind.

"Course I remembers."

"Will you go with me if I decide to leave?"

Mammy gave a solemn nod.

"I'll be beside you ev'ry step of the way, child. Where you go—there I'll go."

With that assurance Amity seemed placated.

"And Serena, too, if she wants to go along," she promised. "I'd miss Serena something dreadful."

"She'll want to," Mammy whispered with surety.

"You. . .you've heard talk, haven't you, Mammy, about servants being liberated by the Yankees? Mammies leaving the children they've raised up? Field hands runnin' off to be free. And—"

"Let them go," Mammy dismissed with a haughty sniff. She sank her bulk on the edge of Amity's feather tick and folded the slim girl into her strong embrace.

"Come what may," she said fiercely, "I'm going with my people, Miss Amity, and you're my family. Where you are is my home. An' pray God someday maybe yo' be havin' lil' ones, and they'll be Mammy's to love an' to raise up just like I done for y'all."

At the thought, Amity shuddered.

"If Cousin Philomen is determined, Mammy, we're leaving the very mornin' after he'd make such intentions clear."

"I'll be prepared, honey, any time you give the word. Miss Ophelia, she warn't your mama's blood, not like you are. And Mist' Witherspoon, he gave me to your mother, girl. Yo' mine, an' I'm yo's an ain't no one—an' no two sides to a squabblin' nation—that's goin' to come between us. An' I promise you that, as the Lord is my witness."

five

Amity's reprieve did not last long, for the next day Philomen Emerson arrived. He seemed delighted to make Amity's acquaintance, and it was clear to her that her reputation preceded her, for she could detect that the Emerson family had done their best to stress her attributes as a potential matrimonial possibility for their homely but pleasant relative.

When Cousin Philomen took Amity's hand in his and squeezed it in a way that she realized he hoped would express the admiring optimism he felt, she shuddered.

He was not a repulsive man, as she had feared, but there was nothing about him to set her heart afire with so much as a flicker of the heady attraction she felt for Jebediah Dennison.

Philomen, who had inherited acreage near his Uncle Raynor's plantation, was short, balding, plain, and, perhaps because of all he'd seen and endured while at war, humorless. He had a dour expression that in his better moments was merely bland.

Amity found it disconcerting to make an amusing remark and have it go unrecognized by Philomen.

Even worse was when such comments drew a perplexed glance from him, as if he couldn't understand what she had meant by such a statement.

Philomen had long since concluded that ladies were a confusing lot, so when he was met with a situation or remark that was beyond his ken, he smiled agreeably and inquired no further.

Amity knew that there could be no understanding between them, and her heart rebelled against being borne along, like a leaf carried in a stream. She refused to allow herself to be married off without protest.

The Emerson kinfolk did all that they could to place the pair regularly in each other's company. Over the days and weeks that followed, Amity realized that Philomen was a cordial and pleasant man who possessed a kind nature and a well-intentioned heart.

Due to the living conditions he had endured while fighting in the War for Separation, Philomen had a poor constitution. The fact that he didn't dwell on his aches and complaints raised Amity's opinion of him.

Amity came to view Philomen as a gentleman she could never hate, but neither was he a beau she would grow to love. He hadn't the ability to stir passion within her and was bland as unsalted corn mush. For just that reason, Amity felt alarmed whenever Philomen's looks grew more adoring. He was content with a mere crumb of attention from her.

Philomen tried to please Amity and cheer her up, an attribute she appreciated most when bad news arrived from the war. Word had been disseminated via an Atlanta newspaper that Ol' Joe had been replaced by Major General John Bell Hood, just as Confederate soldiers had predicted on the veranda of the Sheffield home weeks earlier.

Casualties had risen sharply for both North and South, as Hood, not a patient man, recklessly attacked Yankee positions, gaining only a bloodbath for his men. Ophelia and Amity discovered their pa's name on the list of the wounded, and Ophelia's husband, Major Emerson, was among the missing and unaccounted for.

Because Amity had lived with Ophelia's difficult temper and trying nature, she desperately wanted to protect Philomen's feelings. It was evident that he had already suffered much in life. She wanted to keep him as a friend while refusing him as a suitor, but she was not sure how realistic a goal that was.

"What yo' think o' Mist' Phil?" Mammy presumed to ask one night as she helped Amity get ready for bed in early July.

Mammy's question made Amity grow thoughtful. It was an issue she had already discussed with Serena, who, as an uninvolved third party, confirmed Amity's reactions to the Emerson relative who was spending more and more time with his kin that he might also be close to Amity.

The girl stared into the looking glass and carefully laid down the brush with which she'd been working her honey-colored tresses.

"Philomen's pleasant, kind, gentle, intelligent, industrious, upright. But he's. . . ."

Amity gestured with hands palm up in a display of inarticulate confusion. Words to describe her swirling, confusing feelings failed to make the journey from mind to tongue.

"But not for you, child?" Mammy finished softly as she took up the hairbrush that Amity had abandoned.

Amity gave a sigh of relief at being so understood.

"No. He's not the man for me," Amity murmured. She lifted her eyes and met Mammy's dark gaze in the vanity mirror.

"I didn't reckon yo' be thinkin 'bout marryin' Mist' Philomen," Mammy admitted, sighing. "Miss Ophelia, she be marrying for whatever de reason she had for snagging Mist' Schuyler, but I knows my lil' Miss Amity, an' when she be marryin' it'll be for love alone, no matter what de gemp'mum's sentiments."

Amity frowned, studying the husky black woman's fathomless face.

"Have you heard something, Mammy? Something

that you believe I should know about? And don't deny that you usually know more about what's going on in a household than the folks who own it. I know you hear plenty as you move around the mansion on catfeet, with family members unaware of your passing presence. Something's on the tip of your tongue. Tell me what it is, Mammy."

Mammy paused with the boar brush midstroke. She gave a huffing sigh.

"Mayhap be I jus' have heard a somethin'," Mammy admitted. "Business concernin' a right private matter."

Amity was aware that the study was the usual scene for confidential conversations.

"Were you listening at a closed door?" Amity asked, her voice stern, but her eyes laughingly conspiratorial as she realized how Mammy had probably come by her knowledge.

Mammy gave an unchastened chuckle.

"Seems like as if just perhaps I was dustin' the fancy work on Mistah Raynor's study while he had a visitor there makin' a request o' him. So then I moved on to clean the portrait o' Mist' Raynor's great-grandpapa hangin' nearby in de hallway."

Such details began to drive Amity to distraction.

"Mammy, please! Don't do this to me. Be out with whatever it is you have to say. Don't keep me in suspense, Mammy. What did you learn?"

Mammy began dragging the brush through Amity's heavy hair, as if the familiar motion made the uncomfortable news a bit easier to share.

"Now that we's got Misses Lavinia and Maybelle's nuptials behind us, Miss Ophelia be gettin' mighty antsy to get yo' betrothed to Mist' Philomen, married up, and entrusted into another's care. An' if I know Miss Ophy, it be a'fore winter be comin' on—as I think she's considerin' how many mouths they be to feed an' how much money can be saved."

Amity stiffened at the reminder that the Emersons might view her as a burden.

"That's Mister Raynor's concern, not hers."

Mammy gave a vigorous nod.

"Deed it is, Missy, but yo' know how Miss Ophelia can be. And now Mister Raynor is off to town a goodly amount, same as Mist' Philomen, an' somebody's gots to attend to the managin' o' this plantation, what with the fiel' hands runned off, an' Miss Ophy, she seems like she's considered that she be the mos' likely."

Amity's heart tightened as she considered what her domineering sister might be capable of doing in an effort to trim the costs of running Magnolia Manor.

"Exactly what did you overhear, Mammy?" Amity asked, her voice steady, although she quailed inwardly. "Word for word, now, if you please."

"Well, a few days ago I heard Mist' Philomen and Mister Raynor talkin' in the library when they gots home from military drills wit' neighborhood gemp'mums. They was discussin' lots o' things, but among them, Mist' Philomen asked Miss Ophelia's papa-in-law for yo' hand, seein' as he's the man of the house and yo' be livin' under his roof."

Although she had known what plans were afoot, Amity gasped. Her heart momentarily stopped before it escalated to a frenzied rhythm that made her limbs feel weak and her head swim.

"Mammy, no!"

"Oh, yes," the slave answered in a grim, resigned tone. "But Mist' Raynor, bless him, he tell the young gemp'mum that he thinks he'd best be a-speakin' of that to Miss Ophy, since Mist' Schuyler's wife be yo' next of kin, not him. Mist' Raynor said it not be in his place to make such a serious answer on behalf of another person, especially 'bout such a monumental prospect as matrimony."

Amity drew a deep breath.

"And has he? Has Cousin Philomen spoken to Ophelia?"

"Not to my knowin'," Mammy said. "Nor to Serena's hearing, neither," she added a bit sheepishly. "I shared the secret wit' her so's she could help me be alert an pr'tect you."

"Good," Amity sighed relief. "Philomen's a nice

man, and I hate to think of ever hurting his feelings by having to turn down his proposal, but feeling as I do, there's no way I could marry him. I'll just have to discourage him from daring to ask.

"Why, Mammy, the idea of marrying him, going to live at his plantation, and being expected to let him. . . ." Amity's soft words dissolved into another shudder.

The idea of residing with Cousin Philomen as his bride left Amity cold and shaken, whereas the thought of sharing such unspecified closeness with Jeb Dennison had caused the most thrilling dreams to consume her.

"What are we going to do, Mammy?" Amity whispered when she realized that listening outside her door could be one of the Emerson servants, as loyal to their charges as Mammy was to her. If word got back to the Emersons about this conversation, Ophelia would not take kindly to having her intentions thwarted.

"There's always Mist' Witherspoon's plantation, Lambie," Mammy reminded in a hushed voice as she cast the door a dark look.

Amity gave a low and bitter laugh.

"Don't think that I haven't given that thought. But I'm afraid to try. You've heard the menfolks talking, Mammy, and you're aware of what Mister Raynor says when he returns from the home guard drills.

Why, he's after us constantly not to go out alone and not to wander any distance from the house.

"There are bands of marauders, and to the shame of the South, the Rebs are pillaging the countryside the same as the blue-bellies, commandeering starving folks' last food, heartlessly robbing them of their treasured heirloom possessions, being rowdy toward the womenfolk other gentlemen have fought and died to protect. And—"

Mammy sighed and gave a troubled nod.

"Yes'm, Miss Amity, I've heard. I know it's dangerous. But—"

"Why, if we met up with the likes of them, I'd. . .," Amity shook her head and fell silent, unable to voice the unspeakable horrors that would await them in the course of their desperate journey. By comparison, Cousin Philomen no longer seemed so unappealing.

"It be like yo' heard Serena say," Mammy reminded, "we's the Lord's—leastways Serena and I is—an' yo' could be, iffen yo' turn yo' life and heart over to the Lord and trust an' allow Him to guide you. Iffen yo' be doing exactly what the Lord wants yo' to do, Lambie, then He keep you safe on yo' mission, no matter how desperate it be.

"An' iffen for some reason you ain't kept safe, then it only be 'cause de Lord be lettin' it happen that His glory will be seen. He can take plumb awful situations and grow 'em into miracles when He uses folks who've got seeds of faith inside 'em and seek to live not for theyselves, but to live for Him, hidin' theyselves in Him, like the Good Book says."

"I don't know, Mammy," Amity said.

"Yes yo' do!" she retorted. "Serena, she's been a-tellin' me how sometimes late at night yo' helpin' her with her readin'. She gettin' plumb good, that girl is, 'cause she be telling me what chapters of Scripture she been readin' and what ones you read to her when the words got too diff'cult. So don't be telling me that yo' don' know, 'cause I knows yo' starting to understand the Good Book in your head, Lambie! But we's prayin' that soon yo' goin' to start understanding it wit' your heart."

"Mammy, I've got more important things to worry about right now that the Bible, interesting as it sometimes is," Amity pointed out.

"Yo' ain't got nothin' more important than yo' faith, Miss Amity, and yo' eternal future. But the Lord, He don't put no pressure on yo' to decide iffen yo' going to love an' trust Him. He lets ever'one make up their minds free an' unhampered. So'll it be with yo'.

"But I wants yo' to think about what yo' ol' mammy is a-sayin' so that yo' know that no matter what happens, de Lord is there and He be a-waitin' on yo'. Yo' don' have to face nothin' alone, honey, even if I should die and be unable to stay by yo'. With the Lord dey ain't nothin' yo' can't face and endure. Even marriage to Cousin Philomen. And he is a decent sort. I suspects he be a Christian from things he said. Though I know that when that special spark is missin', that don't seem to be enough."

"It's not," Amity said. "I want more—so much more. Whatever are we going to do? I like and respect Philomen, and I hate the thought of rejecting him and hurting his feelings, but I won't be pushed into marrying a man I don't love. The thought of leaving terrifies me. And if we decided to, how would we best go about it?"

"Carefullike, I reckon," Mammy finally spoke. "I suspects if we all was to light out all o' the sudden, Miss Ophy'd know where we were goin' to," Mammy sighed. "If she's determined to marry yo' off to Mister Philomen, then she'd be het to fetch us back. She might even order Serena an' me whupped."

The thought sickened Amity.

"I'd never allow that. She'd have to whip her way through me to ever get to you or Serena. But it seems we don't have a chance to escape," Amity said, her tone dismal. "At least not right now."

"Maybe the tide will turn."

"Perhaps," Amity murmured. "But until then all that we can do is bide our time and hope for the best. Even if Cousin Phil does talk to Ophelia and she dares to give in to his request that we marry, I can postpone the ceremony almost endlessly."

"There be ways for that awrighty!" Mammy said and gave a conspiratorial chuckle.

"He's a shy man," Amity pointed out.

"Could be that he'll be a spell before he gets up the gumption to ask Miss Ophelia if yo' can be his bride. He was plumb hesitant broachin' de matter with Mist' Raynor, and him the uncle who's been like a papa to the boy. So I 'spects that it may take him a while to get around to speaking to Miss Ophelia. Praise God for dat, 'cause it gives us time in which to lay our own plans in de matter."

"Yes," Amity agreed. Then her eyes widened as an unsettling thought occurred. "Unless Ophelia decides to take the matter in hand and raises the matter with *him*."

Mammy's eyes widened as she realized the likelihood of that outcome, for Miss Ophy was shameless when in pursuit of her desires.

"Miss Ophy a pow'rful woman," Mammy said. "But she, too, is in de Lord's control. He can restrain her if it serves His will, so that she'll be found makin' a diff'rent choice, not even sure, herself, why she is. She thinks she's in control, but she ain't, 'cause God is. Ain't nothing in this ol' world that happens without de Lord knowin' about and allowin' it, as He always has since de first moments of creation."

"Really?"

"Yes, Lambie. Ol' Mammy wouldn't lie to yo'. Why, when the world was a new place, de Lord, He knew already that one day I'd be standin' here big as life talkin' Scripture to yo' and tellin' yo' to trust Him. And the Lord, He already knows if yo' gonna choose to love an' accept Him or if it be yo' choice to reject Him. Serena an' me, we hopes yo' make the right choice when the moment of decision comes."

"I hope so, too," Amity murmured, even though she wasn't confident that she would recognize such a moment when it arrived. Although she was well-educated in comparison to her slaves, she felt totally unschooled in areas of faith where the household servants had a deep, practical knowledge.

"I meant to tell yo', too, Lambie, that yo' been a-pinin' for that Mist' Jeb y'all met in Atlanta, believin' yo' won't never see him again. Well, don't yo' trouble yo'self about that, 'cause if it's the Lord's will that yo' do, sure as can be, yo' will."

"And if I'm not meant to see him again?" Amity inquired, her voice cracked with emotion.

"Then de Lord will give yo' the strength and wisdom to accept that situation, trust Him, and know dat it's for de best."

six

Even though the Emerson family and their house guests had been warned to be watchful for the arrival of Yankee soldiers and had scared themselves with talk of their coming, deep down they had believed they would be spared. But it was not to be.

Days later blue-bellies were everywhere. Neighbors sent runners or someone brave enough to ride out on spavined old mules to warn of the Yankees' approach.

The frightened residents of Magnolia Manor scarcely left the solidly built house except to hide possessions from Yankee raiders as well as from Rebels who would ruthlessly commandeer valuables for the cause even if it meant leaving Southern civilians to face a bleak winter of starvation and material hardship.

The Emerson kin and their house guests were thankful that the plantation was as far from the Macon and Western Railroad as it was, and even Ophelia had begun wondering if perhaps they wouldn't have had a safer haven at Grandpapa Witherspoon's, although there had been reports of random skirmishes in that vicinity, as well.

Almost daily, thick, oily smoke plumed into the sky, signifying that another elaborate antebellum structure had been razed. Chimneys stood like skeletons against the skyline as the Yankees torched dwellings, leaving their inhabitants homeless.

There were no local newspapers to spread the history of events, but the Georgians had only to look northerly to see the horizon glowing like an ember in the night sky and realize what was happening. The dreaded Yankees were surrounding Atlanta and had ventured south to Jonesboro and Lovejoy as well.

On September second, shortly after the midnight hour, Georgians from as far away as Jonesboro heard massive explosions and surmised that a Southern munitions train had been destroyed to prevent its capture by the Union Army.

Before noon of that same day, Yankees had entered Atlanta, the heart of the Confederacy. Mayor James M. Calhoun and a contingent of the city's gentlemen met the invading force. The city leaders waved a white flag in truce, begging for mercy on behalf of the residents in the captured city.

But Sherman was an officer without mercy. He and his army rolled over the land like some monstrous, inhuman entity consuming and routing everything and everyone in its path.

It was a full fortnight before those in the vicinity of

Magnolia Manor ventured out, and then they did so only as necessary. The womenfolk went out only in the company of an armed man who was grim, watchful, and at the ready. By then they were hungry for news, a look at the latest casualty lists, and any facts that would help them determine their future.

Come mid-September, Ophelia, who was determined to travel to the village and try to discover the fates of their pa and her husband, made the trip with Cousin Philomen serving as her protector.

Lavinia, Maybelle, and Amity nervously awaited Ophelia's return. They hastily arose when they heard wheels crunching gravel on the lane leading toward the mansion, and they rushed to the window, sighing collectively when they saw Philomen's rickety wagon rather than hordes of raiding soldiers.

"What did you find out?" Amity asked as Ophelia entered the house. "Is Papa—"

"Wounded. In a hospital," a weary Ophelia crisply informed. "But he'll live, barring the misfortune of putrefying infection causing him to become septic."

"And Schuyler?" Maybelle and Lavinia questioned in unison.

For an instant Ophelia faltered. She squeezed her eyes shut, struggling to maintain rigid control. Her trembling lips scarcely moved as she uttered the word, "Captured."

Faint shrieks escaped from the Major's sisters.

"But Cousin Philomen assures me that Major Emerson may be better off in a Yankee prison camp than he would have been fighting in or around Atlanta," Ophelia stated. She seemed to be trying harder to convince herself than to give optimistic thoughts to her kinfolk.

"Do you really think so?" Lavinia murmured. "You know what it's like at Andersonville and Libby. Prisoners there don't fare well, I've heard. The way the Yankees have plundered our Confederate Nation, we've little enough for ourselves, let alone to share with the enemies in our prisons."

"Cousin Philomen says that at Point Lookout, Schuyler has more to fear from disease than from the Yankees. And," Ophelia drew herself up straight, "my husband has a strong constitution. Cousin Phil said that there's been talk of another prisoner exchange. We can't be gloomy girls; we must hope for the best. It's what Schuy would want. We must be brave for his dear sake if we can't find reason to manage it from the depths of our own piteous grief."

"You're right," his sisters agreed and fell to their sister-in-law, smothering her in comforting hugs.

"Let's speak of more pleasant things." Ophelia turned to Amity. She seemed to physically shake off her gloom as she would whisk off a cloak.

"You'll never guess who I saw while I was in town today," she trilled.

"I shouldn't hazard a guess, as I know so few people in these parts," Amity said.

Ophelia decided to make a game of imparting the information.

"One of your old beaus who used to come to call."

"There were dozens," Amity reminded and offered a careless shrug. She felt herself blush when she saw Maybelle lift an eyebrow, and Lavinia whispered a remark about Amity remaining unwed, a state of affairs that challenged her claim to having been so popular.

"Since you can't guess, then I'll tell you: Will Conner!"

"How nice!" Amity cried, even as she felt a stab of disappointment that the name had not been that of Jeb Dennison. Warm memories of Will washed over Amity, and she tendered a dozen rapid questions about Will's health, his family, his arrival in the area, news of home, messages from mutual friends, and information about how Grandpapa Witherspoon was faring.

"One at a time," Ophelia laughingly stipulated. "I knew you would be brimming with more questions than I could probably answer in one breath."

Forcing patience that she did not feel, Amity primly seated herself near the hearth where a low fire glowed to remove the damp chill from the cavernous parlor.

"Is Will on furlough?" Amity began.

"No. He's with a detachment of soldiers who are bivouacking in this area. It seems that when Atlanta's fall became imminent, troops began moving south to protect the railroads. Sherman circled around the city with the intent of capturing the Macon and Western line. There's been some terrible fighting, although Will hasn't been involved in anything except light skirmishes."

Amity felt relief.

"Then Will's well?"

"Looking marvelous, actually, considering what he—what all of them—have been through."

"Did you see any of the other soldiers who had stopped by the house to dally of an evening? Any of Will's friends with whom we became acquainted?"

"Not that I recalled, although I supposed there could have been one or two I had met before. They tended to cluster around you since initially I was spoken for and later I was wed," Ophelia reminded and gave Schuyler's sisters a quelling glance, upholding family pride by confirming that Amity had been as sought after as she had claimed.

"Oh. I thought perhaps you'd have recognized others."

"Maybe under better conditions, Amity, but Will's the only one who spoke to me. In butternut brown homespun and unkempt, all Johnny Rebs tend to look the same."

Amity's heart skipped a beat when she realized that there was still a slim hope that Jeb was nearby, a member of Will's detachment. Could it be possible that he was mere miles from Magnolia Manor? Dare she hope that they would one day see each other again?

Amity considered what Mammy had said about the will of God, the purpose for each life, and how if it was in God's plan she and Jeb meet again, they would, but in God's own time.

"Until this moment, I hadn't realized how home-sick I have been to see a familiar face and talk to an old friend," Amity mused, fluffing her fair hair around her wistful face.

"I'll admit that I felt the same when I saw dear Will Conner standing there."

"I wish I could have seen him."

A knowing smile appeared on Ophelia's lips.

"Perhaps your wish will come true, my dear," she said. "I gave Will permission to come calling on us. And, as an old family friend he's got the right, although I did make it discreetly clear that he would be greeted as an old family friend and neighbor of Grandpapa's, not received as a beau. Since you've been—well, you know how Cousin Philomen feels. We do have his sensitivities to consider."

"Will never was a beau. He's more like a brother,"

Amity said. "Will's always been a family friend, and I hope he always shall be."

"That's all he will ever be," Ophelia agreed. "It is all he can be," she warned, and a knowing smile played on her face, deepening the crow's feet that crinkled at the corners of her eyes.

"Exactly what do you mean you by that, Ophelia?"

Pausing to let suspense build, Ophelia smoothed a fold in her faded calico gown.

"Cousin Philomen was good enough to see me to town and back today. En route home, Amity dear, he addressed some business of a personal nature, as I have been anticipating he would," she explained, carefully picking at an imaginary piece of lint on her sleeve. Ophelia bought more suspense by adjusting the brooch on her dress and taking time to wind the ornate timepiece.

Amity's heart leaped within her chest, then felt as if it stopped. Heaviness pervaded her being, and her pulse sounded a death knell.

"Well?" she questioned.

"He's asked for your hand, Amity dear, and I have affirmed that his intentions are honorable, that he will provide for your welfare, and that he is a man to be relied on. I have given him my permission to ask for your hand which, of course, you will be honored to accept."

"Ophelia. . .no. . . ." Amity's dazed whisper was

drowned out by Maybelle and Lavinia's excited chatter.

"In Papa's stead, I have granted Cousin Phil the opportunity to offer you his proposal of marriage. I have also intimated that your answer will be to accept with honor and great pleasure. That foreknowledge should do much to encourage Cousin Philomen not to be dilatory in making his request."

"Of course she will accept!" Lavinia chirped. "He's a real catch. She probably couldn't do better."

"Cousin Philomen's so shy and sweet, Amity. Don't you dare trifle with his heart and keep him on tenterhooks until you agree to be his bride!" Maybelle gaily warned. "And there's no need to postpone a wedding. Philomen's home to stay, you lucky girl. Why, we can have you two married just as soon as we can decently arrange the details and plan a party."

"This is just what we need to chase away the gloom from the awful fighting, the horrible blue-bellies' recent presence, and the depressing news that Atlanta's fallen."

They rushed toward Amity in a swirl of skirts, and their arms twined around her as they bestowed joyous hugs and showered impulsive kisses on her hot cheeks.

"You'll be content with a man like Cousin Phil," Lavinia assured.

"And won't we have fun when the war is over, and

our men are home? We will all live nearby, and. . . ."

The rest of Maybelle's speech was lost on Amity. She felt herself being pulled down into an eddying whirlpool of unhappiness, swept along against her will.

Stunned by the news, weakened by gnawing hunger, Amity felt the room tilt and whirl about her. She struggled to keep her balance but was powerless to stop the movement, too disoriented to counter it.

"Goodness, she's swooning!" Lavinia cried. "Quick—help me! Get the smelling salts!"

seven

There was a flurry of activity as Amity crumpled to the floor. Schuyler's sisters shrieked in alarm and stood rooted in horrified dismay, of little help. As was her nature, Ophelia took charge, her tone brusque and snappish.

"Mammy, fetch the smelling salts from my reticule!" she cried and impatiently shook her sister.

Amity groggily blinked and then turned her face aside and moaned. The world continued to spin around her like a child's top gone out of control, causing her to feel disoriented and sick to her stomach. She went hot, cold, then feverish again, before a consuming chill overtook her. The gabble of the other women's voices sounded from a distance.

Serena carried Amity to the worn horsehair settee and wafted a palmetto leaf fan over her.

"What. . .where. . .?" Amity asked as she tried to sit up, not sure how long it had been since she had collapsed.

She sank back on the velvet throw pillows and remembered with horror that she was now destined to become Philomen Emerson's bride.

"Won't Cousin Phil be proud as a strutting bantam rooster to learn how utterly he has swept Miss Amity off her feet?" Lavinia teased.

"Cousin Philomen has succeed where many other beaus have failed," Ophelia assured. She gave a tittering giggle. "It would seem that the Sheffield belles are especially partial to the Emerson beaus."

"Before Amity swooned I believe she was inquiring about when this wonderful event is going to come to pass," Lavinia reminded them.

"Why, I can remember how eager I was when Papa told me that he had given my Gaylord permission to seek my hand in marriage. I'm sure Miss Amity is as excited as I was. She must want to know how long it will be before Philomen will arrive with his hat in hand, prepared to go down on bended knee to seek her hand in marriage."

"Well, it won't be tonight," Ophelia said in a regretful tone. "Cousin Philomen mentioned that he and Papa Emerson have patriotic business that cannot be postponed.

"But that's perhaps all for the best because earlier in the day, Will Conner—the old family friend Amity and I have been talking about—inquired if he could come calling. As eager as he seemed to see us again and to be received into the parlor of proper people after having to live off the land, I shan't be at all surprised if he doesn't favor us with a visit this very day."

"How wonderful!" Lavinia cried. "It seems ages since we have entertained company—especially a charming gentleman."

"Although staples are precious, we will have our cook prepare something especially lovely," Maybelle promised.

"You might have her ask our Serena for her recipe for tarts," Ophelia suggested. "Mammy will know exactly which little tasty tidbit it was that Mister Will was most partial to when he would come to call, and if we possess the ingredients, Mammy can prepare it for his enjoyment."

"Today started out so damp, grim, and gray, but it's become quite lovely," Lavinia declared. "Think: a wedding in the offing and tonight the first company we've had come calling in ages! Things are looking up, girls."

To Amity they had never looked more bleak. Although she kept a careful smile fixed on her features and hoped that her misery wasn't visible, she knew that Mammy understood and was reviewing possible options that would allow them to escape the fate Ophelia had planned for them.

As much as she wanted to see Will Conner and enjoy being in his company, Amity hoped even more to arrange to speak with him privately. She needed to press him for any news regarding Jeb Dennison and perhaps ask his opinion regarding which way to run, should they choose to flee Magnolia Manor. She would swear Will to secrecy and hope that out of respect to an old friend, he would honor her request and plead ignorance if later questioned.

The other members of the household prepared for the evening with special zeal, even though several times Ophelia hastened to remind them that there was a chance Will wouldn't be able to come calling.

Amity prayed that he would arrive exactly as anticipated. If he didn't come calling at Magnolia Manor that very evening, she would be unable to see him at all, for she had decided that when Mammy helped her undress for bed that night, she would give her servant notice to prepare to flee. There was no time to waste.

Soon after the next day's dawn, Amity was going to leave Magnolia Manor and escape an unwanted marriage. Granted, she liked Cousin Philomen, but in her heart, irrational as it was, Amity loved Jeb. Without his having ever told her his feelings, she also believed that Jeb loved her.

If she was destined one day to meet Jebediah Dennison again, she couldn't bear to be introduced as the wife of Philomen Emerson. Instead, she would wait for Jeb the rest of her days. Better to pine for a true love than to live in comfortable harmony, adjusted to a man not really meant for her by the God

her servants had assured her had a special plan—and
a special man—just for her.

eight

That evening shortly after the supper hour, Will Conner arrived astride a mule he had borrowed from a superior in his detachment. He had promised that he would return early with the beast after a hasty visit with old family friends who resided at a plantation in the area.

As Will made his way up the winding lane sheltered by towering trees, members of the Emerson household flocked from the mansion to greet him. Ophelia ordered a servant to catch the bridle of the beast Will rode and take control of it, freeing him to immerse himself in the attentions of his eager hostesses.

Amity hung back demurely, knowing that if she appeared too forward, she would risk drawing criticism from Schuy's sisters and Ophelia. Inwardly, Amity was thrilled to see Will. His presence at the plantation momentarily took her mind off her troubles.

While Amity was still determined to leave the plantation the next day, she was disturbed by a conversation she had overheard between Raynor

Emerson and Philomen. The two men had talked in low, disgusted tones of Confederate deserters from whom southern women were no more safe than if they confronted an enemy Yankee. Such southern men would callously burn out their own people and would view a woman alone, or in the company of her household servants, as a diversion to be used and then cast aside.

Amity knew that there were also bands of roving Yankees who were going ahead of the Union Army in order to pillage the land and holdings of plantation owners. Nothing was safe from these hordes. They would enter a house and hold the women and children at gunpoint while they searched for valuables.

As dire as her fate would be if she were set upon by a band of southern deserters, Amity's imagination failed her in chronicling the possible horrors that would be her fate if she were to encounter Yankees.

As Will was ushered into the once stately home that had begun to fall into ruin and disrepair because of the wartime hardships, a spark of hope warmed Amity's heart.

Will would be honest with her. He could be trusted to keep a secret. Somehow she had always known that about him. From what Will had been saying about his life since he and his detachment had moved south of Atlanta, he was familiar with the area.

Somehow she would get a chance to question Will

in private. If there was a safer way to travel to Grandpapa Witherspoon's plantation, surely the kind and gentle soldier would know of it and advise her accordingly.

The grandfather clock incessantly ticked off the seconds of each passing minute as Amity patiently bided her time. Her mind searched for a plausible excuse to slip off with Will. She needed only enough time in private with him to find out about Jeb Dennison's health and whereabouts and to discuss her flight to Grandpapa Witherspoon's plantation.

Amity felt weak with anxiety. For months life had been out of her control. Her choices had been forced on her by others. Suddenly she could see a way to make her own decisions and provide a better environment for Mammy and Serena.

The end of Will's visit was drawing near, and still Amity hadn't been able to speak with him alone. She steeled herself to appear calm and casually made a suggestion with what she hoped was the right amount of indifferent politeness.

"I really should show Mister Will around Magnolia Manor while it's still daylight and before he has to leave," she said, covering a delicate yawn. "It's truly a pity that Schuyler or Mister Raynor aren't here to do the honors so that they could have the pleasure of showing him their acreage and enjoying his company."

"I would love to see the property," Will said.

Amity was grateful that Will seemed to sense her desire for a few private moments and was assisting her in her efforts. She rose gracefully. Will stood and, with a courtly bow, offered her his arm.

Mammy had slipped into the parlor.

"I'll go wit' you," she murmured, offering to serve as a chaperone. To prevent the appearance of a servant taking charge, she carefully qualified the remark. "Unless Miss Ophelia would rather go along. Or Misses Lavinia and Maybelle."

Amity didn't dare glance in Mammy's direction lest someone catch a conspiratorial look pass between them.

"My slippers are only now starting to dry out after my venturing into town this morning," Ophelia dismissed, much too ladylike to complain in front of a gentleman caller about her true reason for declining: corns and bunions.

"I'm afraid I feel a touch of grippe coming on," Maybelle excused herself, not wanting to seem too eager to spend time with a young gentleman in the absence of her husband. "This dreary weather may be the death of me yet. Pity the poor soldiers who can't get in from the rain." She drew her shawl about her and gave a theatrical shiver.

Lavinia patted her neat coronet into place and gave a gentle, long-suffering sigh.

"Yes, I do think of our brave boys, especially at times like this when I'm too comfortable to move," she murmured from her place close to the fire. "Were that everyone in the world could know such moments as this all the time."

There were low murmurs of general agreement as Amity, Will, and Mammy made their way toward the front doors that opened onto the wide veranda of the Emerson home.

"Those tarts that Serena showed our cook how to make are wonderful. I shouldn't have taken the last one," Maybelle said to no one in particular. "It was thoughtless of me, considering the daily plight of our guest." She favored Will with a quick, regretful smile that caused him to immediately offer assurances that his needs had been more than met.

"Don' worry yo'self about it, Miss Maybelle," Mammy politely enjoined. "Serena saved a few of her tasties to send back with Mist' Will so he can enjoy 'em on his way back to de camp. An' mayhap share with a few o' his comrades if he chooses."

Will visibly brightened over the prospect, although his expression never lost the grimness brought on by his experiences in the war.

"Much as the idea pains me after enjoying your charming company and delicious dainties, I'll be havin' to take my leave," he said to the ladies.

"Get my wrap, if you would, Mammy," Amity

said, smoothing her voluminous skirts after she passed through the doorway of the parlor and stood in the foyer.

Will turned back and courteously began tendering goodbyes to the matrons still congregated around the cozy room. He explained that he would like to tarry but had to be heading back to his detachment. It was foolhardy for a soldier from either side to be out alone after dark in case he chanced into roving bands of enemy soldiers.

"I'll be takin' my leave after Miss Amity shows me around y'all's lovely plantation," he said. "And I do hope that perhaps I can return to savor your company again before our regiment moves on—none of us having any idea how long we'll be in these parts. We could leave tomorrow, or we might be here for a few weeks.

"Even our officers don't seem to know. I reckon it depends on what the blue-bellies are up to. But, if I'm here, I would beg your permission to come calling again. This has been most enjoyable, seein' y'all."

"It's been our pleasure," Ophelia said, smiling.

"Oh, do hurry back!" Lavinia encouraged.

"You're welcome any time," Maybelle agreed.

"If you have gentlemen friends who would like to spend a pleasant evening, feel free to come in their company, Will," Amity made it unanimous. Her heart skipped a beat when she considered that maybe Jeb could have—would have—come calling if he'd had an express invitation.

"Give our greetings to anyone who knows us," Ophelia reminded. "And give them news of Papa and Major Emerson, of course, for I'm sure they'll be interested."

"By all means. Consider it done," Will politely agreed.

Amity's heart was thumping as she headed for the front veranda with Will in her wake, her steps as light as her soaring heart now that she knew she was moments away from being able to discuss Jeb with a trusted friend.

For the first time since Ophelia had delivered the stunning news of Cousin Philomen's intentions, Amity's heart felt at peace. She stood still so that Mammy could slip a cloak over her slim shoulders and tie its ribbons beneath her pert chin.

As they left the main house, Mammy took her position a pace or two behind her young miss and her gentleman caller. The pair walked down the path toward the various outbuildings, a grove of trees, an overgrown meadow, and then to a bower formed by decorative bushes.

Mammy trailed behind Will and Amity, keeping a distance sufficient to allow privacy to talk, but not so far away that Ophelia could complain about impropriety.

"I'm so glad that you came calling tonight, Will, and that you agreed to accompany me for a walk around the grounds so that we could talk," Amity said in a fervent tone. "I've been almost wild with distraction, hoping—praying—for this time alone."

"My pleasure, Miss Amity," he assured in a gallant tone. Will stood at a safe distance from her, for he had heard enough about Cousin Philomen that evening to know about the expected engagement.

"I'll admit I've been wantin' to speak with you, too," he added, "an' not have everyone there to overhear it."

Amity quailed, wondering if Will was preparing to tell her that Jeb Dennison had departed this life after entrusting Will with the responsibility of sharing the details of his passing with the woman they both knew would care. But it couldn't be that! She decided to take her risks and speak honestly, hoping for the best.

"I so wanted to see you before—" Amity swallowed quickly. "Before I leave. For I don't know when I will see you again, and you have been a cherished and trusted friend to me since we were both small children and I met you at Grandpapa Witherspoon's barbecues and cotillions when our family visited him from Atlanta."

"I possess many fond memories of those days at

home, Miss Amity, as well as of those evenings when you bestowed upon me your gracious hospitality and charming company in Atlanta. While I could have sought you as my belle, I wished to always keep you as a friend rather than to risk more and end up with less."

"Oh, Will!" Amity said, blushing. She was pleased to know the depth of her friend's admiration.

Will gave a hapless shrug.

"You sometimes toyed with suitors' hearts," he reminded in a teasing tone. "But it would appear those coquettish days are over. From what I've heard this evening, am I to discern that congratulations will soon be in order?

"Seems that Miss Ophelia's been hintin' that you'll be marryin' soon. An' Major Emerson's sisters seemed to be a-tossin' out a few sly remarks, too. With all of 'em mentioning a Philomen Emerson and speakin' of him in the highest of regard, it sounds like you've done well by yourself and have at last found the right man to marry."

Amity sighed.

"There's the threat of that, yes."

Will halted abruptly beneath a sweet gum tree and stared at Amity in amused shock.

"Threat?" he whispered, stunned by the choice of words made by a young woman who always tried to be the epitome of tact.

Silence spun between them and tears filled Amity's eyes.

"Threat?" Will repeated the word. "Somehow, pardon my makin' the observation Miss Amity, but that doesn't sound like the words of a happy bride-to-be who's head-over-heels in love.

"Why, for my part, if a woman I wanted to take as my bride considered me a threat, I'd be wounded to the core. And I'd probably decide to love her enough to free her to be with another than to wish to bind her to myself."

Amity squirmed with misery. She smoothed her hair away from her troubled face. Finally, she lifted her sad eyes to Will's face.

"That's because I'm not happy, nor am I in love with Cousin Philomen. Nor will I ever be."

"What's the matter?" Will was concerned, his voice gentle. "Don't you even like him a little bit? From what I've heard sometimes merely likin' someone a great deal is a wonderful foundation upon which to base enduring love that comes later."

"I don't even really like him. I'm in a position where I find myself tolerating him for others' sakes."

"Your sister and her husband's family seem to think the sun rises and sets on Cousin Philomen. But appealing as you are, it seems to me, Miss Amity, that you could have had your pick of beaus. Why him if you don't even cotton to the fellow? It'd be awful to wed a person you didn't like very well."

Amity dabbed at her eyes with a threadbare linen handkerchief. She tried to smile.

"Actually, Will, I was probably wrong. Or in my unhappiness exaggerated. I suppose I like him well enough. In fact probably quite a lot. He's certainly not an offensive, abrasive person. He's rather easygoing and comfortable enough to be around. But it's just that—"

"Ah," Will said, and his tone took on sudden clarity of understanding. "But likin' and bein' comfortable with's not love."

"Exactly," Amity said, knowing that Will Conner would understand what she meant and how she felt. "Philomen's not the man I'd have chosen to marry. He's a kind man. I know he'd never harm me. But to wed such a boring and unimaginative person would cause me to die a little every day.

"I'd—well, to be unabashedly honest, Will, feeling as I do I'd almost sooner marry a lively, interesting, and passionate blue-belly than such a bland, plodding Southern gentleman."

Will gasped.

"Surely you jest!"

"I'm sorry, Will, I suppose I didn't mean that. At least not about preferring a Yankee. But Cousin Philomen is so predictably dull and so lacking in passion or imagination, that I already feel frustrated by him. I know it would only become worse if we were married.

"Maybe it wouldn't be so bad, but I can't resign myself to marrying him, adjusting to his personality, consigning myself to a lifetime of tending his household, and seeing to his needs. Not when I. . . ."

Amity's courage failed her.

"You can't fathom becoming Philomen's wife when you love someone else?" Will finished for her. "Is that it? Because you've already given your heart to another?"

Amity gave Will an almost defiant stare. His lips curved into a faint, knowing smile.

"Yes," she whispered. "Yes I have. Not because I intended to, mind you, but because somehow I was helpless not to."

"That's what I thought."

"But how did you know that?" Amity asked, hoping that Will didn't misunderstand and believe that it was *he* whom she professed to love above all others.

"Because I saw you on the veranda the night before y'all fled Atlanta for Magnolia Manor, Miss Amity. Don't forget that I was in Jebediah Dennison's company that night, and for many nights after. I saw what was in your eyes, my dear, and I know what's in Jeb's heart."

At the mere mention of his name, Amity's heart

quickened, and her hands trembled.

"Pardon me if I'm speakin' out of turn, Miss Amity, but could you be pinin' for Jeb? Or have you met another?"

Amity knew that for the sake of decency, she should demurely turn away from what was becoming an intimate and inappropriate conversation with a man, but she couldn't. Her heart—her love—demanded that honesty be served.

"Yes. I suppose that, well, unreasonable as it may seem after such a brief encounter, I am in love with Jeb. I do pine for him, Will. And it's been my sweetest dream to believe that he longs for me, too, that he cares as I do. If God is willing and miracles happen, perhaps someday he and I could be together."

Will nodded.

"Then I was right, for I thought so, and in the time that's passed I've witnessed Jeb longin' for you, even though he'd never had the chance to whisper sweet words of love in your ear.

"Something special occurred that night in Atlanta, Miss Amity. Something powerful passed between you. You know it. Jeb knows it. I know it. And the way he almost wears out the pages of the Good Book in his knapsack, I think he's seekin' godly answers—perhaps a miracle—so that you might see each other again."

"I want that more than I want life!" Amity passionately proclaimed.

"Is Miss Ophelia aware of your feelings? Do Major Emerson's sisters know your heart in this matter?"

"No. Only Mammy's aware of how I feel. And Serena," Amity admitted.

"Jeb would be a mighty happy man to know that his feelings are returned. I know that he's unceasingly prayed for that—and for you."

"Then you have seen him? Recently?" Amity asked, her excitement knowing no bounds.

"Up until two weeks ago we were together almost constantly," Will affirmed. "We got split up during a minor skirmish with the Yankees over toward the road leading to Mist' Witherspoon's plantation.

"I think Jeb might've been wounded, I'm sorry to say. Shelling was such that I wasn't able to return to him, nor, if he was unharmed, was he able to locate me. I hated to move on without him, but I had no choice."

"Oh, no!" Amity cried.

"If it'll make you feel better, he wasn't on the ambulance laden with injured. For my own peace of mind, I checked. And I've read casualty lists. His name's not appeared on any of them, so there's hope."

"Oh, I hope so," Amity breathed.

"Jeb might've gotten separated and linked up with

some other Rebs. I sure hate to think of that; Jeb an'
I got pretty good at communicatin'. I got so's I could
read his gestures.

"That failin' he'd write a bit on the back of casualty
sheets that we carried with us and used to tuck
beneath our clothes to break the bite of the early
autumn wind. He had a right neat hand. I expect that
he was an educated fellow."

As Will talked on, Amity understood what Jeb's
life had been like since she had last seen him in
Atlanta. She felt grateful relief to know that Will had
made Jeb's life easier, and that in return, Jeb had
been a true friend. If only there hadn't been the
skirmish that had parted them.

"I miss him," Will admitted. "Jeb was always
someone to visit with, an' he never tired of listening
to me. But then, perhaps that's because he usually
saw fit to keep me talkin' about *you*, Miss Amity. I
expect if I know somethin' about you, Jeb Dennison
now treasures that knowledge as well."

"You talked about me?" Amity asked, surprised
but pleased.

"About you, Miss Amity. He couldn't hear enough
about you. Other Johnny Rebs would be around the
fire talkin' about their wives or their intendeds or
simply reminiscing about the belles they'd courted
back home. Jeb, he seemed to hunger for the same.
Don't reckon he's had many belles to court, him

bein' a mute an' all.

"Jeb would write questions on the back of casualty sheets, and I'd answer 'em as best I knew, talkin' till I tired, or until I could no longer think of stories from our childhood at your Grandpapa's plantation. That seemed to satisfy Jeb, considering that I've known you an' your kin for as long as I can remember. I know that bein' close to me somehow made Jeb feel as if he was closer to you."

"What did he ask you?" Amity murmured, realizing that she wished she could learn the same kind of information about Jeb.

"Oh, lots of things. So long as I was talkin' about you, Jeb was happy. Why, I can pro'bly tell you *exactly* what he asked," Will exclaimed and began reaching into voluminous pockets, pulling out tightly folded casualty sheets.

"Maybe I'm still carryin' some of them that Jeb wrote on. With damp, cold days comin' on, sometimes I'm called on to help in startin' a fire, so I carry a wad of casualty sheets with me."

"Oh, I hope you haven't already burned the sheets that he wrote on," Amity said, her heart aching as she considered that an accident of selection could have robbed her of precious contact.

Will frowned as he scrutinized the wrinkled, fraying papers.

"Here's one. An' another. This's one, too, although it ain't all there, I'm sorry to say. But 'twill serve as better than nought."

Soon there was a small sheaf of papers with smeary charcoal writing still visible for Amity to hug to her heart. Upon seeing proof that her deep feelings were returned, Amity knew a pang of happiness unlike anything she had experienced since the moment on the veranda in early summer when she had lifted her eyes and seen Will approaching with the man of her dreams.

Amity stared at the papers bearing Jeb's script as if to memorize them. She was loathe to return the papers, but before she could offer them back, Will bid her keep them.

"You've told Jeb all that you know about me," Amity said, "so can you tell me all that you recall about him?"

"He's from an area north aways, far closer to the Mason-Dixon line," he began.

Will sketched in a story of a man not too different from himself, a young gentleman whose life had been on an even course until the War for Separation disrupted his plans.

"Naturally, him bein' a mute an' all, I don't know all about him that I'm sure you wish I did. But I can vouch that he's an upright soldier," Will assured. "Intelligent. Kind. Compassionate. Brave. Decent. Ethical. Amusing, though he can't crack jokes.

"He's the kind of fellow I've been glad to have beside me in the trenches, although I can tell that totin' a rifle doesn't appeal to him, while helpin' to heal mankind does. I guess that's because he's a Christian. Judgin' by my own familiarity with the Good Book nowadays, I'd say that Jeb Dennison lives his faith."

"You said at one time that you believed his papa was a physician."

"I was wrong," Will said. "It's Jeb himself, I gather, who's had some medical trainin'. He was schoolin' up North—Harvard, I think he said—when the war broke out. So obviously he came home to be with his own people, fightin' side by side, as many of our boys bein' schooled in the North did when the time came to have to plumb loyalties and make a choice."

"A doctor who can't talk?" Amity mused, then shrugged away the problems such a situation might present.

"May be that he ain't always been that way," Will said. "I never asked him. He could've lost his voice from an injury. Scars bear testimony that he's been through his share of difficulties at the hands of the blue-bellies."

"Yo' best be gettin' back, Miss Amity," Mammy approached them and ducked her head, giving Will a warm smile as she reluctantly intervened. She did not want to arouse the suspicions of Miss Ophelia and her sisters-in-law.

"Yes, Mammy," Amity agreed.

Carefully Amity refolded the precious casualty slips bearing her beloved's scrawl, and she turned toward the mansion.

"So what are you going to do?" Will asked. "If I may be so bold as to risk offendin' your sensibilities by askin'. It seems you're committed to one man while truly lovin' another. That's not an easy plight in which to find yourself. I know you Miss Amity. What're you proposin' to do about it?"

"Do?" Amity inquired.

"You'll marry one man while lovin' another?" Will's expression revealed that he couldn't believe that the belle he knew so well would ever accept such a situation.

"I don't want to," Amity admitted carefully, not yet prepared to take Will fully into her confidence. "But I don't know what I'm going to do to prevent it."

He nodded, misunderstanding her intent.

"Yes, an' you might never see Jeb again. An' from what they've been saying, Mister Philomen will provide for you. Maybe you'll even come to love him the way a wife should, given time and kind treatment and consideration."

Amity shook her head.

"No, Will. Never. And I'll never marry Philomen Emerson."

Will gave a rueful smile.

"Y'all seem plenty determined, Miss Amity," he said. "But I recall that Miss Ophy can get pretty single-mindedly het up, too, when she's settin' store to accomplish somethin'."

"I will not be marrying Philomen!" Amity said, her tone adamant. "I decided that months ago. Now's simply the time for me to see my options through to fulfillment."

"Options?" Will echoed.

The moment had come to risk complete honesty with her childhood friend and hope that the future would uphold her belief that he would never betray her.

"Mammy, Serena, and I are going to leave Magnolia Manor."

A flash of alarm crossed Will's features.

"Does Miss Ophelia know this?" he asked.

"Of course not. We're going to run away. And if you breathe so much as a syllable about it to anyone—I'll never forgive you, Will Conner, for as long as I shall live."

Will looked more amused than alarmed by Amity's bold plans.

"Your secret is safe with me, Miss Amity. You know that. If questioned, I will profess ignorance of your intentions."

"Thank you. Is there any way you can help me, Will? I'm thinking about going to Grandpapa's plantation. He would take care of us."

Will was a long time responding.

"I can't actually assist you in your escape, Miss Amity. While I feel loyalty to you, of course, my first obligation is to the C.S.A. I can't be away from my regiment to escort you, unfortunately, for I would if I could. But I can tell you what I know about troop movements. How best to travel. What to look for to keep yourself as safe as possible. I wish I could offer more."

"That's a start," Amity sighed in grateful acceptance.

"When are y'all leaving?"

"Soon. Very soon."

"Good. Then the information I can share will at least be current. It's ever-changing out there," he said, giving a gesture that swept in all directions.

Amity listened intently as Will told her what she and her household help could expect as they made their way from the Emerson property toward her grandfather's plantation.

"There are both Yankee and Rebel detachments in the area," Will warned. "At night, you may not be able to tell which you are nearing. So be careful when you travel. You may not see soldiers because you haven't trained yourself to be alert. They will know you're in the area long before they see you."

He cautioned her about making an undue amount of noise or using campfires.

"I'll remember," Amity promised, and nodded to encourage him to speak further.

"Sometimes the safest thing might be to forego walking across the countryside. You might want to consider floating down a creek on a raft at night. It would be perilous and unpleasant, but it could be safer. If y'all lie still on a raft, you'd have a better chance at traversing the area undetected."

"We can manage that. Thanks for suggesting it."

"And iffen y'all do have to skirt close to regiments that are camped, check for Quaker guns. They're a dead giveaway it's a Rebel unit, not Yankees."

"Oh, Will, I know the difference between a pistol and a rifle, but that's about the extent of my knowledge. I'm afraid I wouldn't know one rifle from another."

"You don't have to, Miss Amity. You'll have no problem recognizing a Quaker cannon." A bitter smile came to Will's face.

"We Reb's are poorly armed, you know. So we have to do what we can to contribute an illusion of strength. When we dig in foxholes and rifle pits, we saw down trees with straight trunks, lop 'em off to appropriate lengths, and insert these logs along the rifle pit. From a distance it's hard to tell if it's a log or a cannon barrel. Yankees don't use Quaker guns, but we Rebs have no choice."

"Oh, Will," Amity murmured.

"And if you see a wheel of buzzards hoverin' in the sky, try to avoid the area. It probably marks a battlefield where some unfortunates' bodies lie molderin' in the sun. Y'all don't want to pass too close and have enemy forces discover you if they're lootin'. And y'all don't want to end up gettin' contaminated with a sickness, either."

By the time Will had finished giving Amity all the information that he felt she should know, her head was fairly swimming.

"You're determined to go?" he asked.

Amity gave a grim nod.

"I have to, Will. I can't stay here."

Will nodded understanding of her plight.

"That's what I thought. Well, good luck, Miss Amity, and Godspeed. If Mist' Witherspoon's plantation happens to be burned out, you're always welcome at the Conner estate. Mama and Papa would be delighted to see y'all and help out as they can.

"I'll rest easier knowin' your mind, and where you're goin'. That way, if Jeb and I happen t' link up again, I'll be able to share with him the sweetest knowledge he'd ever extract from me: where to find the woman he loves."

"Oh, Will, I'm so grateful I could hug you!" Amity cried.

Laughing contentedly he opened his arms to her.

"I should like nothing better, my brave and beautiful friend. Jebediah Dennison is a lucky man, possessin' the heart of a woman like you."

"Until we meet again," Amity breathed as she gave Will one last hug.

"Go in peace, Miss Amity. And God bless and protect you."

Will turned and strode toward the borrowed mule as Mammy and Amity lingered so that she could compose her emotions and hide her precious papers. Jebediah's hands had touched the pages that she now pressed close to her heart. His written words conveyed a faithful love that his mute lips could never express.

nine

Had Amity had her way, she would have fled Magnolia Manor the next morning without giving any thought to preparation. But Mammy and Serena, who as slaves had had far less secure lives than Amity, raised questions about their journey that made their mistress aware of the danger they were walking into.

They would need food to sustain them, enough clothing to shield them from the elements, and sufficient time to get safely away before their absence was noticed.

If evening came before anyone realized that something was amiss, the women would have placed a full day's travel between themselves and Magnolia Manor. If their disappearance were discovered before noon, however, Mister Raynor or Cousin Philomen could hitch up a mule and locate them with embarrassing ease.

Once they had agreed on the most viable plan for their escape, they rehearsed the details several times until they were calmly familiar with their plan. When morning came, all three were certain that they could leave on a supposed task without raising anyone's suspicions.

The next morning, Mammy, Serena, and Amity met at a predesignated spot, giggling with relief that they had managed the first step of their plan and were about to set off on an adventurous journey of escape.

Their laughter was short lived. Mammy and Serena were well aware of the fate they would face if they were separated from Miss Amity and caught by angry southern men who would wish to make an example of them. The two slaves dropped to their knees and prayed fervently.

Amity, after a moment's consideration, smoothed her skirt and sank to her knees beside her two servants. She felt humble and hesitant as she offered her own requests to the God that Mammy and Serena trusted so completely.

And so they began their journey. When it was safe, they traveled narrow country roads and winding trails. When they approached civilization, they shrank into the underbrush where briars, brambles, and prickly bushes snagged at their clothes and hair.

After Serena came within inches of stepping on a poisonous copperhead snake, the trio tended to step lively and squawk with alarm over the least movement near them in the woods.

By sundown they were exhausted, but they vowed to continue trudging on, thanking the Lord that there was a full moon to guide their steps. It made travel easier as they wound their way along the ribbons of roads cutting through the countryside toward Grandpapa Witherspoon's plantation.

Physical exhaustion finally forced the women to halt, even though their spirits desired to keep going. They huddled together for warmth, wondering if they had been missed yet and if Philomen and Mister Raynor had pressed the local militia members into service to come looking for them.

It was with relief that they set out again after several hours spent in fitful sleep. By nightfall of that next day they felt that success was possible. By the next morning, they believed success was in their future, although they admitted that they had been through a grim and grueling three days. Amity had only to glance at Mammy and Serena to know how grimy she, herself, must appear.

Although the journey had left the trio bone-weary, famished, thirsty, and suffering from an assortment of injuries from blisters to scratches, there was an air of adventurous frivolity. Any time their hearts were faint, they were revived when they realized the glorious truth. They were free!

Amity was freed from an unhappy future, and Mammy and Serena had escaped from the house that had never felt like home. Where Miss Amity went, they, too, were free to go unquestioned, for they were in a white woman's company.

There was a bond between the two servants and their mistress. Amity was theirs just as surely as they belonged to her, and recognized that they were the Lord's and that He was seeing them through their sojourn to a new and happier land.

"I can't believe we're almost there," Amity said.

"Well, we is—an' we ain't. We's close, sho' nuff, n' the worstest is behind us, but we won't make it to the big house by nightfall," Mammy clarified.

"Oh," Amity breathed her disappointment at not being able to retire to a comfortable bed after soaking in a bathtub brimming with hot water.

"We can't show up on Mist' Witherspoon's door-step with yo' looking like po' white trash, an' Serena an me looking like no-account field hands instead of valuable household servants. We's goin' to make ourselves look respectable first," Mammy insisted.

"How? By bathing in a downpour?" Amity asked, as she cast a worried glance toward the slate gray clouds that looked swollen with autumn rains as they tumbled across the sky, their ominous movement accompanied by distant thunder.

"We're goin' to stop fo' the night at a lil' cabin not far from here. It's on Mist' Witherspoon's planta-tion, but quite a piece from the house. We can haul water from the creek and sponge off, change frocks, an' wash these filthy clothes."

"It will be heaven to don a clean, dry frock," Amity said. "If only we could have a hot meal, too."

"Not unless they's some way to make a fire in the hearth, honey, an' somethin' to cook in. Otherwise we'll jus' have to nibble down what I's been pickin' along the way an' eat it as the Good Lord saw fit to provide it for our needs."

"I wish we hadn't had to leave most of our clothes at Magnolia Manor," Amity murmured.

Mammy sighed, as did Serena. It was the younger servant who spoke.

"It seemed the only way we could travel fast, Miss Amity, an' the way to best convince Miss Ophy an' the others that mayhap we wasn't really going to visit Mist' Witherspoon for a spell."

Mammy gave a rowdy laugh.

"If they believes Miss Amity's note after the way we all left, they's gullible, though it be the hones' truth! With us a-travelin' so light an' not arrangin' for Mist' Raynor nor Mister Phil to fetch us over to Mist' Witherspoon's and leavin' strangelike as we did, I'll bet they's goin' to be lookin' in the wrong direction. They'll think Serena and me are runaway slaves.

"'Stead of comin' to look for us at Mist' Witherspoon's plantation, bein' as we all left almost on the heels of Mister Will, they mayhap be a-thinkin' that Miss Amity done run off to be wit' Mist' Will, goin' after him like one o' them shameless camp follower wimmen!"

"Jus' so we have time to safely get to where we's goin'," Serena said. "Dat's all I'm askin'."

"Mammy, is it much farther?" Amity asked an hour later as the daylight waned and a smacking drop of icy rain landed on her cheek.

"It's right up ahead, Lambie. I believe's I can see the door from here! Be thankful it be a-standin' yet. I wasn't so sho'. It's been a long spell since this plantation was my home."

"Thank goodness!" Serena cried when she saw the rustic, dilapidated overseer's shack with its sagging roof and weather-beaten walls.

"Hurry!" Mammy gasped as she broke into a trot and urged Amity to pluck up her skirts and run, too. Lightning struck nearby, creating a thunderous boom, and Amity and Serena screamed. With frightened cries the women hurried toward the cabin.

They had scarcely stepped beneath the eave's sheltering overhang when the clouds opened and rain battered down.

"In just the nick of time," Amity said. "Thank God for shelter when we needed it."

She looked around her. Dust and cobwebs hung over most of the shack, but in the dim light it appeared that other areas had been swept smooth. The surface grime had been disturbed—and recently.

"Someone's been here," Amity said in a whisper. "Wonder who?"

"I don't know," Amity said and shivered from the dampness of her clothes and the specter of Yankee forces nearby.

"Sho' nuff they be gone now," Mammy said, but with less conviction in her tone than Amity liked.

"Well, this is plumb snug after what we's been growin' accustomed to," Serena said in an obvious attempt to bolster their lagging spirits. "What's the big house like, Mammy? Has it got a large kitchen?"

"Indeedy it does," Mammy assured.

Mammy moved around the cabin, locating a dented enamel basin and a few rusting pots. She opened the sagging door enough to set the dishes under the eaves to collect rainwater so that the three of them could wash themselves. While they were waiting for the water to collect, Mammy spun tales about the splendors of Mister Witherspoon's mansion.

" 'Course dat was before the war," she reminded. "But I 'spects it's still a home to do its people proud. We'll get cleaned up tonight an' eat what roots an' berries I've collected in my bag an' what fruit we found unharvested and hangin' in trees at abandoned, burnt-out plantations. When comes the dawn we'll light out to go the rest of the way to Mist' Witherspoon's home."

"How long will it take?" Amity asked tiredly.

"An' hour walkin' slow, honey. Who knows how quick if we're all to step high an' lively?"

With heavy rain moving in after the initial wave of thunder had passed through, the cabin grew so dark that they had to squint. Mammy struggled to her feet, dug through one of the bags she had carried, and produced a stumpy candle and matches.

"We's almost home," she said, "so we don't have to ration the candle so close." She struck a match, then deftly touched it to the wick. She held the match to the bottom of the candle, melting wax into the center of the table, then plopped the candle into the drippings and waited for it to cool and hold the taper upright.

"There! That be better."

"It's almost homey," Serena said.

"After three nights in the woods, this is like a castle," Amity conceded.

None of them raised the question of what they would do if Mister Witherspoon's plantation had been burned out, its inhabitants scattered to the four winds. In low voices they talked. Suddenly, they heard a creak overhead. The startled women stopped talking. Their eyes enlarged and they stared at one another, not daring to breathe.

"What was that?" Amity finally asked in a strangled whisper.

Serena and Mammy exchanged worried glances.

"It sounded big enough to be somebody," Amity whispered. "What if it's a Yankee?"

For a moment there was nothing but strained silence—and the faint groanings of pressure against boards in the attic.

Mammy hove to her feet and pulled Serena up with her.

"They's somethin' in that attic, sho' nuff, but I'm a-bettin' it's only a mama opossum an' her brood. Hopin' it ain't a skunk." She attempted a feeble laugh.

"I'm goin' to investigate," Mammy said. "De Lord didn't bring me this close to taste failure. Help me up on dis ladder, Serena." Mammy grabbed the rung, instinctively moved to slap dust and grit from her hands, then stared at them as she seemed to realize that the ladder steps had been scraped clean by something. . .or somebody.

Mammy climbed a step. The ladder groaned under her bulk. She lifted her other foot and stepped on another riser. Her head neared the attic opening.

"Serena, han' me dat candle," she ordered. "But keep the matches in yo' hand 'n case somethin' snuffs it out."

Serena eased the candle from the table up to Mammy. The older woman held it aloft and stared.

"Well, I'll be!" she gasped, amazement evident in her tone. "There's a gemp'mum up here!" Then she emitted a squawk that sent her dropping down the ladder and caused Serena and Amity to cling together in fear, desperate prayer on their trembling lips.

"Mammy, what's up there?" Amity cried.

Mammy's eyes were big as saucers.

"Dey's a gemp'mum in the attic," she said, "a-laying still as death. An' it's either dat mute man, Mist' Jebediah, or I be seein' his ghost!"

"Mammy, are you sure?"

"I never been so sure in all my born days!"

"Give me the candle," Amity said. Only the thought of seeing Jeb again gave her such courage, but as she lifted her head into the attic space, her bravery wilted.

"Oh, my," she breathed.

Mammy was right. It was Jebediah Dennison. But Mammy was wrong, too, thank God, for Jeb wasn't a dead man, though he soon would be if someone didn't do something right away.

"He's sick, Mammy. Very sick," Amity said. She wrinkled her nose as the odor of putrifying wounds wafted toward her. "We've got to do something, but I don't know how we'll get him down from the attic. It's very close quarters."

"You leave that to Serena an' me, Miss Amity. Yo' jus' clear us a space to make a pallet fo' him, an' we'll do the best we can."

The three worked with desperate haste. Amity chewed her lip as Mammy and Serena disappeared into the attic. The joists groaned beneath their weight. Amity was aware of their success only because of the thumpings and scrapings.

She wondered that even a mute didn't cry out in pain as they unceremoniously wrenched him from his resting place. In a moment Mammy came down the ladder, huffing for breath, and when Serena lost her balance and accidentally dumped Jeb into Mammy's arms, Amity saw why—Jebediah Dennison was unconscious.

"We's got to have some heat. This man's not only got an infected wound, but a fall cold a-comin' on."

Mammy ordered Serena to break up what was left of a rickety chair and build a fire in the grate.

"An' hope that the flue ain't plugged with a bird's nest."

When Serena had successfully started a fire, Mammy quickly gave her another order.

"Yo' fetch in one of them pans o' water, an' start tearing off lil' pieces of roots an' things so we can make a broth. We's got to get somethin' hot inside Mist' Jebediah to give him the will to fight, or he's not long for this world."

Amity hardly heard Mammy's orders, so intense were her prayers to God, a God she dared to trust to keep Jeb safe and well, even if theirs was not a love meant to be. Even if the fact that Jeb would live on might mean one day he would go to another woman and find love.

"Is there anything I can do, Mammy?" Amity asked, wringing her hands.

"Nothin' I ain't already doing. Jus' keep on prayin', Lambie, and know that Serena and I is, too."

Two hours later, Mammy finished spooning hot broth between Jeb's lips, stroking his throat to encourage him to swallow. She pronounced that he was better and that with luck, he would live until morning.

"We'll have to go to the big house an' fetch help to move him there," Mammy decided. "Mist' Witherspoon'll know what to do. Dawn be comin' early. So y'all had better rest up now."

"I'm too addled to think of sleep, Mammy," Amity said. "You lie down and Serena, too. I'll stay up and tend to Jeb."

"Alright, Lambie. I am plumb tuckered. An' I know that Mister Jebediah couldn't be tended with any hands more lovin'."

ten

Amity passed one of the longest nights of her life as she kept her vigil beside Jebediah, who groaned and writhed in his sickness. Several times during the night, she was terrified that he was going to breathe his last, and she prayed to God to preserve and protect the man she loved.

When the first rays of dawn crept over the horizon, Amity's eyes were gritty from lack of sleep, and her body felt leaden and dull from exhaustion. But Jeb seemed a bit stronger than he had the night before, and hope flamed anew.

Amity was loathe to leave Jebediah when Mammy and Serena sleepily awoke and quietly began discussing their immediate plans.

"I know yo' wants to stay with yo' loved one and nurse Mist' Jeb, Lambie, but dat ain't for de best. We's gots to think of all o' our needs. But don' you fret. Serena, she's took care of sick folkses. She knows more about healing than yo' do. She knows almost as much as I do."

"I know, Mammy."

Mammy looked at Jeb and then laid a kindly hand

on his forehead.

"I'd like to stay wit' the boy an' tend to him myself, but yo' need me to guide yo' to the plantation, and dey'll need me to lead 'em back to help Mist' Jebediah when they fetch him to the big house."

"That's true," Amity said, bowing to Mammy's logic. "But we'll have to hurry. Maybe if you went by yourself, I could stay with Serena."

"The way things be, Lambie, neither Serena nor I dare be caught walking the lands alone. Someone might collect us as runaways. An' it be fittin' that yo' be there to greet your grandpappy when we arrive, 'stead of me arrivin' alone."

Amity reluctantly realized that Mammy's plans were the wisest course of action.

"Then let's hurry, Mammy," Amity said. "I'm ready to go. The sooner we get home the quicker we can get help for Jeb."

So eager was she to reach the plantation that Amity knew no exhaustion and only slowed occasionally when she realized how Mammy labored to breathe. The older, heavier woman was walking with quicker steps than usual so she wouldn't lag too far behind her young mistress.

"It's not far now," Amity said, pausing to look around her. "I recognize that grove of trees from one time when I went riding with Will when we were children. We'll be home soon."

"Dat's right, child," Mammy panted. "We's about to the fambly cemetery."

"Oh! I see it!" Amity said, feeling a burst of relieved enthusiasm when she suddenly realized that they were closer to the big house than she had realized. On Witherspoon land, she hoped that she could rush ahead a bit and that her trusted servant would be safe if she was left behind in Amity's eagerness to be home with her beloved grandfather.

Amity strained to catch sight of the big house between the cover of leaves that still remained in the towering trees. So intent was she on assuring herself that the house still stood that she didn't bother glancing into the small burial plot enclosed behind a rusting wrought-iron fence.

Mammy did, and she quailed when she saw the mound of fresh dirt rising above the tangled, dead grass. Mammy, who had made many sad trips to the cemetery to observe the committal of the folks she had loved, tended, and prayed for, slowed her steps. As she passed the gravestones, memories flooded over her along with the names and the dates inscribed on the headstones.

"Won't Grandpapa be surprised to see us?" Amity called. "Oh, do hurry, Mammy! I know you're tired, but if you could keep up with me, we would be there sooner. Maybe they will have a cart you can ride in for the return trip to Jeb. I can't wait to see Grandpapa. I know he's going to be thrilled to see us."

"I sho' nuff hope so, honey," Mammy said in a soft, unsure tone. "I sho' hope so."

Amity darted ahead before she could see the worried cast enter Mammy's dark eyes, and she didn't notice that the older woman's frown had intensified to reflect an added burden of concern.

Amity quickened her pace as she made her way through the meadow, climbed over a fence that kept her from the lane leading to the Witherspoon lawn, then made her way across the expanse of house yard before she rushed up the flagstone walk, the heels of her shoes clattering. The house—the entire plantation—seemed unnaturally silent.

Mammy caught up with her mistress and banged the ornate knocker down hard on the solid front door a few times. There was no answer, so she repeated the action. She had just lifted her hand to repeat the gesture when the door creakily swung open.

Mammy tiredly dropped her arm to her side as a hollow-eyed, frightened servant peered out.

"Who yo' be?" she asked when she saw Mammy. "An' what yo' be wantin'?"

"Denizia?" Mammy asked. "Is that you?"

The woman frowned, her expression hesitant.

"Yes, dat be me, but what yo' wantin' here?" Fear haunted the haggard woman's eyes.

"Nizy, it's Mammy, home with Mist' Morgan's lil' girl, Miss Amity. We's come to see Mist' Buford Witherspoon iffen he still be here, an' stay with ya'll for a spell."

The woman stood as a statue.

"Don't yo' recognize me, 'Nizy? Yo' titched in the head, girl? Say sumpin'!"

The words jolted Denizia out of her daze. She shook herself, seeming to cast off the strange mood that had overtaken her, and stepped forward. Her tone warmed with welcome.

"Mammy! Of course I recognize you now. I jus' wasn't expecting to see you." She rubbed her eyes.

"Still cain't believe I'm seein' yo' again. In recent times we's known such unhappiness that I couldn't believe the joy. Was afeared yo' was an apparition, I was, and that if I'd be seein' yo' ghost, Lord pr'tect and preserve me from who else's would be comin' to call."

Mammy didn't have time for such considerations. Especially not in broad daylight. She decided to get right down to business.

"The Yankees been here?" Mammy asked. "We was stayin' over at the Emerson plantation, and they was awful in that area, robbin', pillagin', burnin' good and decent folkses out of they very houses."

Denizia nodded. Her sad expression seemed to indicate that she could match every horror story

Mammy could relate.

"They passed nearby. We was luckier an' others. Ol' Mist' Buford, he was all het up to stand de Yankees off all by hisself." A wistful smile washed over Denizia's sad features, and her eyes momentarily sparkled at the memory.

"He got plumb apoplectic an' Big Tom had to calm him down an' put him to bed, same as he had to do dis summer when Mist' Buford took a notion Gen'l Hood could use him up towards where they be fighting to drive de Yankees back from Atlanta. De ol' gemp'mum took off that day, after orderin' Big Tom t' take care of the place in his absence." Denizia gave a hearty chuckle.

"But a mighty tuckered out Mist' Buford come home a couple of hours later, without the strength to take himself to his bed. Big Tom hadda carry him to his quarters, tend to him like a chile, an' poor ol' Mist' Buford didn't leave his bed fo' three days afterward."

Mammy made a tsk-tsk noise with her teeth and tongue.

"That don' surprise me. That do sound like Mist' Buford, sho' nuff. He was quite a grand ol' gemp'mum."

"Where is he now? Is Grandpapa still ailing?" Amity asked, speaking up for the first time.

Denizia looked at Amity with sad eyes, seeing her

owner's kinfolk for the first time.

"Oh no, honey," she explained softly, her voice heavy and velvety with sympathy. "Your grandpappy's not ailin' now, chile, he's dead. He won' never ail no more. An' he was such a dear ol' man, and so good to us darkies what was his, we's hopin' to see him again on dat great gettin' up mornin'!" Denizia patted Amity's arm.

"Don' yo' fret over your grandpapa, Miss Amity. He was a good man, salt-of-the-earth. His passin' be peaceful and he had an expression like he knew he was goin' home to be wit' his believin' loved ones who'd gone on home in faith before Mist' Buford was called there hisself."

For Amity, there was no comfort found in assurances of her grandfather's relationship with God. She felt only the knifing agony of loss and the sensation of being alone in the world.

"Mammy!" Amity cried out and began to sob. "Oh, Mammy! What are we going to do now?"

Mammy was thoughtful a moment, then seemed to center on the basic practicalities of living, for it was certain that nothing could be done for the dead.

She took a deep breath and licked her lips as she bought time in which to think through their basic needs and pray for the answers that would allow them to most directly fill them. She folded Amity into her arms, hugging the girl close as she wept her grief, confusion, and disappointment in all that she confronted in life.

"Well, first off, we's goin' to fetch Mister Jeb an' Serena to the big house," she decided, "an' then see what we can do to help Denizia and Big Tom around dis here plantation."

She paused and gave the premises and surrounding acreage a critical stare. It was more tumbledown than she had expected, and her hopes had not been high.

"Who all yo' got here workin' de fields, Nizy?" She asked, facing Mister Witherspoon's trusted servant who had stood by him when others had fled or sought to betray him.

The raw-boned slave who had tended to Buford Witherspoon stared at her hands.

"Jus' my Big Tom an' me, Mammy. De rest o' 'em done runned off wit' the Yankees. An' me an' Big Tom, we ain't known what to do 'thout someone to tell us.

"We been a-scared, too, in fear dat someone, suspectin' ol' Mist' Buford passed on, would come and take us, an' we wouldn't have no pr'tection. We's aware dat we could go free. But dis is our home. We's allus been free here. Just now we's more free than we was free then."

Mammy nodded perfect understanding, for that was how she felt toward Mister Morgan and Miss Amity, although she felt no such loyalty toward Miss

Ophelia.

"This yo' home as long as yo' wants to stay and tend it and be took care o', I'm sure, because my Miss Amity, she in charge now, an' she's a kind-hearted mistress," Mammy clarified. "She be yo' new young miss, too. An' she take care of yo' like she takes care o' us so good while we's a-doin' our level best of a-takin' care o' her."

"Praise the Lord! We's glad to see y'all," Denizia said, her countenance shining with relief.

The sentiment was echoed by Big Tom when he arrived from the fields. He had heard the voices of strangers and had hesitantly sidled up to the house, keeping to the shadows. He had wanted to know if his wife was in danger before he made his presence known.

When he recognized Mammy, he let out a whoop, sprinted across the front lawn, and scooped her into his massive arms, swinging her around as he cried with glee.

"Yo' remember lil' Miss Amity?" Mammy asked him when he replaced her on the front veranda step.

He nodded enthusiastically.

"I sho' do. She was the purtiest baby on the plantation when her dear mama and Mist' Morgan and his lil' girl from his first marriage come to call."

"And she's the loveliest belle to ever grace this plantation right now, even purtier than her mama."

"Sho' sad that y'all didn't arrive in time for Mist' Buford to see his daughter's lil' girl one last time," Tom said, his voice solemn. "It'd have cheered his ailin' heart, sho' nuff."

"Guess that the Good Lord just didn't mean for it to be," Mammy said.

"Come in and rest," Denizia encouraged, bidding them to enter the mansion with a welcoming gesture as she turned to lead the way.

"We cain't rest but a moment, Nizy. We's got us a heap o' work to do afore we can. Dey's a feller down in that little cabin in the woods. We left Serena, one o' Miss Amity's loyal servants, with him to tend his needs. He been wounded. Gots an infection, I expects. An' a fall cold comin' on, too."

"We'll fotch him to de big house," Denizia said, nodding. "I'll ready another room—"

"We's gon' give him the best care. He's a Rebel, sho' nuff, though he cain't talk nary a word. But we wants to heal him so some day he can go home and hug de ol' mammy who raised him up as a boy and had a hand in turnin' him into a gemp'mum with qualities that Miss Amity was but helpless to love— even wit' him bein' a mute an' all."

"He be Miss Amity's beau?" Denizia said.

Mammy nodded.

"Sho' nuff is. And we ain't gonna let either Miss Amity or Mist' Jeb down. Lord willin', we's gonna save his life so dey can be together. Mayhap with us here.

"This be Miss Amity's plantation now. Left to her by her mama. Miss Ophelia, she warn't no relation to Mist' Buford. She ain't gots no claim to dis here land—nor to us. Mist' Jeb an' Miss Amity could be happy here iffen they'd choose to be."

"I'll be prayin' that," Denizia said. "We don' wants to have to open up another grave in de fambly cemetery. It was a sad task for ol' Big Tom an' me, committin' de master we loves body into de ground as ol' Mist' Buford's Master welcomed him home to the big mansion He has prepared in heaven. Ol' Mist' Buford, he'd had a long, full life. We don' wants to fail Miss Amity so dat her beau goes home and leaves her a lifetime o' loneliness 'til they can meets again."

"Denizia," Amity quietly said. "Please don't talk like that. You're upsetting me. Scaring me."

Mammy put an arm around Amity.

"It's the truth, Lambie, and the truth ain't always pretty to hear. But it be like it was when King David lost his little chile dat he loved so much. He was grievin' and carryin' on. Den it struck him that it be dat his lil' boy, he wasn't never gonna come back.

"But King David, he realized dat he could go to dat little boy in the great fo' ever an' fo' ever be wit' the Lord. So he chose to amend his life, so that he'd be fittin' to meet the Lord and his loved ones who'd gone on ahead. We's got them kinds o' choices, too."

"I know. I've read enough Scripture to be aware of that. But it's hard. Seeing Jeb has only made me more aware of how much I love him."

"As pow'rful as yo' love, Miss Amity, yo' keeps in mind dat de Lord loves Mist' Jebediah more. If de Lord calls him home, it's onliest 'cause de Lord loves him most—and while de Lord can share such a fine man as Mist' Jeb wit' all o' us, he belongs to de Lord what created him."

"Dat's right," Denizia assured. "But don' yo' think we're goin' to be slackers in carin' for yo' beau, Miss Amity. Iffen it's meant to be, de Lord will give us healin' wisdom like we ain't never known afore, so's we can nurse yo' loved one back to full health."

"Nizy's right, Miss Amity. We sho' know what's we want. But the Lord's will be done."

Amity swallowed tears at the back of her throat and gave a quick hug to the two women beside her. They were strong in body but had even more strength of spirit.

"Amen," Amity whispered her acceptance.

eleven

It seemed to take an eternity for Denizia to put a quick breakfast on the table so that the plantation's new arrivals could replenish their strength. Mammy had suggested that Miss Amity rest, but Amity negated that idea, using Mammy's own logic.

"From what Will Conner said, there are roving bands throughout the area. They won't magically detour through these parts because they're on Witherspoon acreage. And if you, Denizia, and Big Tom are stopped, you might be taken into custody by someone, and then there'd be no help given to Jeb. He and Serena would be alone in the woods with no one coming to offer assistance. But if I went along, you'd be under the authority of a white woman."

"Dat's true. Den yo' be welcome to come along— needed to come along." Mammy gave a slow smile. "An' even if what yo' said warn't true, I knows yo' wants to see yo' beau again, to reassure yo'self that he still be among the livin'."

At the idea that Jeb should die before she could touch his hand one last time, Amity's heart galloped with fear. She calmed down only as she remembered what her servants had assured her: If it were meant to be, Jeb would live. If not, then his death somehow served the Lord's will, and when she passed through her grief, she would come to recognize and accept her loss.

Even so, Amity wanted to do what she could to shape the future.

"Really, we must hurry," she encouraged. "The sky's been overcast. We don't want to be bearing a deathly ill man home in a chilly autumn drizzle."

"Dat we don't," Mammy agreed.

"I'll be wrappin' up de leftovers in a cloth so's we can' take sustenance to yo' gal Serena and Miss Amity's beau," Denizia offered.

Big Tom scraped his chair away from the table.

"We ain't gots no mules nor critters anymore," he apologized. "I wish we had a fine and fancy carriage and beast wit' which to go fotch yo' Mist' Jeb. I's been thinking. It be a pow'rful long ways to carry him laid out on a board, even iffen I quicklike construct some handles.

"I's been thinkin'—out in de shed dey's a pony cart that Misses Amity an' Ophelia used when they was lil' girls. Iffen he be a tall man, he gon' be kinda scrunched up, but we can make de trip quicker." He paused and puffed out his chest, flexing his arms.

"I 'spects I can pull about as well as a contrary ol' pony ever did! De cart's sturdy an' light."

Denizia laid a hand over her husband's strong grip

that rested on the table.

"I'll help," she offered.

"Me, too."

"With all of us working and the Lord giving us strength and knowledge, we'll do just fine," Amity assured. "Thank you so much. Y'all are a true comfort to me." Amity could see in their eyes that she was also a comfort to them.

"Of course," Denizia said. "Yo' our new young miss—an' we loves and wants to take care o' yo' an' your'n."

Hauling the pony cart to the woods was a comparatively easy matter. Big Tom hauled it with the zest of a young man half his age. But by the time they loaded the unconscious Jeb into the cart and tucked in the few possessions that Amity and her servants had carried, the conveyance's wheels dug into the ground.

Sweat poured off Big Tom as he breathlessly moved ahead. His eyes strained and his teeth ground as he struggled to haul the pony cart up rises that they had hardly noticed in their haste to reach the cabin.

Even with Mammy and Denizia's help, it was difficult going, and soon Serena and Amity threw their weight against the back of the cart. With a combined effort, the trip to the big house was accomplished. Everyone felt weak and lightheaded when they halted near the door.

"Beggin' yo' pardon, Miss Amity," Big Tom said

and dropped to the ground between the traces of the pony cart. "I cain't walk another step. Iffen I's got yo' permission, I needs to rest a spell afore I can manage to pick up Mist' Jeb an' lug him to the sickroom."

Amity laid a gentle, grateful hand on the big slave's shoulder.

"You take all the rest you require, Big Tom. Thank you so much. We couldn't have done it without you."

He gave her a pleased smile.

"I'll only be a moment," he promised.

"There's no real hurry," Amity said. "Mister Jeb isn't going anywhere."

Mammy clucked and fluttered around Jeb, hoping to begin her sickroom duties even as they were clustered in the front yard. A blue jay swooped and darted, disgruntled at the activity beneath the tree where she had a nest.

A few minutes later Big Tom sprang up, seeming to feel rejuvenated. With Denizia's help, he gently boosted the inert man into his arms. Mammy rushed ahead to open the door, and the Witherspoon servants made their way with their charge, depositing him on the waiting bed in the sickroom off the kitchen.

"Big Tom, yo' shuck him out o' his clothes." Mammy began to snap orders, knowing that as Miss

Amity's mammy she had the authority.

"Denizia, iffen yo' don' mind, yo' het up some water. The young gemp'mum needs a bed bath." Mammy sniffed and her nostrils crinkled. "I do declare, white folkses or not, he be smellin' lack a pole cat! An' dese wounds do need cleaned."

"Right away, Mammy," Denizia said, and seemed relieved to have someone else in charge.

"Serena? Girl, yo' stay here an' give me a hand. I ain't as young as I used to be. I need yo' to help me move him. Even though he's among the livin' yet, he be like a dead weight."

Serena set about her work, having labored with sick charges before in the Atlanta house.

"Now yo', Miss Amity! Yo' hie on out o' here. Tain't fittin' for yo' to be here!"

"Mammy!" Amity protested, though she knew her mentor was right.

Mammy's stern manner relented.

"Go on, Lambie," she encouraged in a gentler tone. "Yo' can come back an' set up a vigil at Mist' Jeb's bedside jus' as soon as we tend to our duties an' make him fittin' to be seen by an innocent an' unworldly belle.

"Now go, Miss Amity. The sooner yo' leave, den it be dat much sooner yo' can come right back an' hol' his hand an' smooth his brow to yo' heart's content."

Amity left with reluctant steps. She paused at the doorway.

"You're all so busy, and being so needed. I wish that there was something I could do."

"They is!" Mammy said. "Yo' can pray fo' Mist' Jeb."

"An' iffen yo' wanting comfort fo' yo'self and the Lord's strength, then yo' can get ol' Mist' Buford's Good Book," Denizia suggested, explaining to Amity where it could be found.

"Mayhap it be a comfort to yo' in yo' loss o' yo' dear grandpappy if yo' young hands be touchin' the pages of the book he treasured fo' all o' his days."

Although Amity was the figurehead in power at the Witherspoon plantation, she did as she was told. Awe filled her as she realized that her grandfather had consulted the Bible so often that its cover was worn and the pages were velvety from use. The book fell open to the passages it seemed the Lord intended her to read so that she would find comfort, assurance, and acceptance.

As Amity read, it became easier for her to give up her own will and instead seek God's direction. Burdens slipped away and cares were relieved as Amity placed herself and Jeb in the loving God's eternal care. She knew that if she had to face Jeb's death, the Lord would sustain her and help her live on in faith, believing that one day she would know unending joy with the man she loved in a heavenly home.

During the next three weeks, Amity was afraid a dozen times that Jeb was hours from death. But due to the strength God gave the three servants and Amity, death was defeated each time. The four worked as a united group of believers, willingly becoming servants to each other in their effort to save Jeb's life. Amity no longer saw herself as above performing chores that other southern women would have consigned to exhausted slaves.

Amity made several trips to her grandfather's new grave, and many times she prayed that Big Tom wouldn't be needed to dig a similar hole for Jeb Dennison's earthly remains.

"Maybe there's nothin' more we can do, Miss Amity," Mammy said. "I've used all of the herbs an' roots that I'm aware can heal folks. Mist' Jeb don't seem to be getting any worse, but he ain't gettin' any better, either, and if he lingers like this, he's goin' to suffer a decline, n' be gone before our eyes. We's got to do sumpin', and will, unless it ain't what de Good Lord plans for Mist' Jeb."

"No! Oh, don't even say that. I can't bear it. I've come to care more for Jeb with each passing day. He won't die—I won't allow it!"

"Then yo's goin' to hafta do something, Miss Amity. Or increase yo' prayers that the Lord will hear your pleas."

"We've got to do something, but what?"

Mammy shrugged.

"Send for a doctor," she suggested. "There was an elderly gemp'mum, a special friend of Mist' Buford's, an' he come here to nurse Mist' Buford's servants when dey took sick an' I know if he's still alive, he'd come to heal this gemp'mum."

"Send Big Tom to fetch him," Amity said, "and have him tell the doctor that we'll pay him soon; I'll get the money somehow."

"Mayhap sooner than you think," Mammy said. "When I was here in my younger days, Miss Rosalyn, yo' grandmama, used to have a jar of silver dollars buried away for a rainy day. It pro'bly ain't still there, but den, so few of us knew o' its whereabouts that could be dat it's a miracle and it still is.

"Either way, it's worth a look. We might find disappointment at the end of a spade—then again we might find the assistance that de Lord knew we'd one day have to discover."

"Send Big Tom for the doctor, and find us a spade, Mammy." Amity sighed. "Grandpapa no doubt dug it up long ago and donated it to the cause. I don't feel that the cause is right myself, but I know a lot of good Christian Southerners have philosophies that somehow allow them to reconcile slavery with the Good Book. That isn't my concern. Seeing to Jeb's health is. I pray that money hasn't been spent."

"Mayhap it ain't, and maybe Mist' Buford didn't donate it to the Confederacy, especially iffen he didn't know Miss Rosalyn had it set back for diff'cult times. He was generous 'nuff wit' her that she could've set back her lil' nest egg without troublin' him to mind to it, as he did the rest of the plantation. They wasn't but a few of us, Miss Rosalyn's most trusted servants, who knew about that jar of money. Might be it's still there."

"I hope so, for I'm so poor that I couldn't spare the pennies to weight a dead man's eyes." Amity drew a deep breath, then pulled away when she realized what she'd said. "Go talk to Big Tom, Mammy. And ask him to please hurry."

When Big Tom returned after going in search of a physician, the towering servant was so winded and weak that he couldn't find the strength to eat. His mission had taken several hours, and he had returned with a young, modern physician who had taken over the retired doctor's practice. He asked questions of the servants and Amity with a lazy drawl that belied his sharp eyes that missed nothing.

"I don' like the looks of him," Mammy said when the doctor left, staring down the lane after him.

"I don't care if he looks like a gargoyle if he can heal Jeb."

"That ain't what I mean," Mammy said. "He's

presentable enough, but there's somethin' about him that I jus' don't trust. I cain't quite put my finger on what it is."

Amity saw nothing out of the ordinary when Dr. Brink stepped from Jeb's sickroom upon his return the next day, pronounced the continued care that they had given him excellent, and offered a professional opinion that with medication Jeb would completely recover. Dr. Brink lined up an array of bottles and tendered instructions to Mammy and Amity on how to correctly administer the potions.

"We thank you, sir," Amity said. "And what do we owe you?"

The doctor looked at her dirty hands, and seemed to consider that Amity been pillaging the pitiful vegetable garden for something to prepare for their evening meal. He appeared to be taking in her almost threadbare frock when he named a low figure.

Inwardly Amity sighed with relief. They would not have to part with any of the large coins left in Grandmama Rosalyn's discolored fruit jar that had been buried for so many years beneath the grape arbor. Such an expenditure would arouse suspicions among their neighbors about how they could have acquired such financial reserves.

"Mammy, run fetch a coin from my reticule," Amity said. "Thank you for coming, doctor, and good day."

Amity felt a prickle of alarm when she caught Dr. Brink's eyes resting on her in a manner much like Philomen's. As a popular belle, Amity had had enough experience to know that the doctor's interest in her was not simply professional.

Dr. Brink licked his lower lip.

"I'll stop back to see the patient in another day or two, Miss Amity. And," he added, "there'll be no charge for my consultation. I'll consider myself paid, and paid well, if perhaps your house girl could have a treat laid out for us and we could share a spot of tea and a bit of conversation."

"I'm sure you have overhead expenses," Amity said, using the word she had heard her papa use when transacting business. "I would like to pay my just debts, and I am able."

"Very well."

Although she knew that she should graciously invite the doctor to tea, as well, Amity simply couldn't make herself bow to social conventions. There was something about Dr. Brink that she did not like—but to bring Jeb back to health she would face anyone.

After Dr. Brink left, Amity scrupulously followed his instructions. Hours later, Mammy insisted that Amity leave the sickroom and allow her trusted servant to handle the sickroom duties.

"Yo' have to let me minister to Mist' Jeb, honey,

before yo' gets sick, too, an' I've gots to take care of you. I don't know how much more these ol' bones can take."

"Very well, Mammy," she agreed.

Even though Big Tom and Mammy freed Amity from many sickroom tasks, she saw a lot of Jeb. As far as she was concerned, she saw too much of Dr. Brink, as well. He came calling more regularly than Amity believed was necessary once Jeb had begun to regain his strength. But there was little she could say to discourage the doctor, for he did not charge for his visits and Amity could hardly be so rude as to refuse his courtesies.

"Jeb's sleeping," Amity said a week later as she exited the sickroom and conferred with Mammy.

Mammy frowned.

"Miss Amity, has yo' noticed a difference in Mist' Jeb?"

"He's getting better. Stronger. His appetite has improved."

"No, Lambie, I mean somethin' *different.* Have you heard him try to talk?"

"Mammy, you know he's a mute!" Amity reminded, giving her servant an unbelieving look.

Mammy was stolid. Her lips folded in a grimace of determination.

"I'm tellin' you, Miss Amity, Mist' Jeb's able to talk. I's heard him!"

"Moans, of course," Amity was quick to agree. "He's been in so much pain. I'm sure even mutes groan in anguish."

"Well, I've heard somethin'," Mammy said, "An' I think that the doctor man, he thinkin' they's somethin' odd, too." Mammy licked her lip, then stared at the floor between her feet.

"An' I don't trust that doctor man, jus' like I tol' you, Miss Amity. The other day when he was checkin' in on Mist' Jeb, he shooed me out of the room an' gave Mist' Jeb some kind o' potion. It made him talk, but he talked real funnylike. He sho' don' sound like all of us when he speak."

"Oh, Mammy," a tired Amity sighed.

"Mist Jeb, he don' remember none of that miracle medicine," Mammy persisted. "An' I's sho' he don' recall it givin' him the capacity to speak, him bein' a mute an' all. But the po' man, he sho' nuff was groggy de next day from dat strange medicine Dr. Brink be givin' him, I been thinkin'."

"So that's what happened to him," Amity mused. "Well, you know how Dr. Brink prides himself on practicing the very latest medicine. I don't intend to give Dr. Brink another moment's consideration. I think with luck we'll have seen our last of him anyway, because he said that Jeb will be well enough to start getting up and around by the end of the week."

"If it ain't already too late by then," a glowering Mammy muttered as Amity departed for her quarters. Mammy went into the sickroom to keep a solitary, worried vigil.

"Now I'm thinking we's got even more tragedies to be a-prayin' don' befall none o' us."

twelve

Jeb was better by the end of the week, and the week following that Amity could see his strength returning almost by the hour. Mammy, deciding that the young soldier could use the mental stimulation and companionship, prepared a daybed for him in a corner of the kitchen near the potbellied stove so that as he felt up to it he could listen to those around him and remain comfortable and warm.

When he was awake, Jeb's expressive eyes set Amity's heart aflutter, and she never tired of asking questions that he could answer by either nodding or shaking his head. But there was more—so much more—that she wanted to know about Jeb.

One afternoon when she had a few moments, Amity explored the attic where she and Ophy had played as children. There she located an old slate and a minuscule piece of chalk.

Jeb's eyes lit up when she gave the slate to him, but he soon became frustrated. There was so much he had to say and so little space in which to write it, and the chalk held between his tightly pinched fingers was quickly disappearing.

Amity developed a system of asking Jeb a question

and then going about her chores while he laboriously wrote his answers on the small slate nestled on his lap. She vowed that she would pillage the attic until she found old papers which they could press into service along with homemade ink and a quill salvaged from the henhouse. A few bantam hens that had been too wild for the Yankees to capture when Sherman and his troops had fanned through the area still made their home there.

Sometimes Amity grew concerned about Jeb when he struggled to phrase what should be detailed explanations as concisely as possible in the crowded space allowed by the slate. She sensed that his frustration was building, and she worried that, as weakened as his state had become from weeks of illness, he was setting back his physical recovery by becoming so mentally overwrought.

"Don't bother with writing out an answer right now," she said one evening and eased the slate from his hands. "You can write the answers when you've regained more strength. That's what matters the most."

You're what matters now ! his eyes seemed to say, even as his hands fell obediently limp over the slate. He carefully set it aside, then his hand encircled Amity's wrist. He drew her down onto the edge of the settee next to him and stroked her cheek with his forefinger.

Amity shivered beneath his gentle touch, and he noticed her reaction. He seemed to draw courage and he drew her face down toward his. Her hair fell forward, brushing across his face as she laid her head on his shoulder while he patted her smooth, soft arm.

Amity sighed, content at last to be in Jeb's arms. His fingers sifted through her wavy hair and explored the flare of her eyebrows, the line of her cheek, the curve of her mouth, the indentation of a dimple, and a beauty mark off to the side of her chin.

Their lips were mere inches apart, and their eyes were locked. Jeb's lips worked, as if he so desperately wanted to say something, but couldn't.

Amity was unsure if she lifted her lips to Jeb's, or if he drew her face up so that their mouths could meet, but an instant later their lips were pressed together in snug perfection.

Amity's pulse thundered, then warm, wonderful, weakening sensations overwhelmed her until she felt too satiated to move. She wanted only for the moment to last for eternity. Never had she been happier or more at peace in her life.

Jeb was short of breath when Amity freed herself from his arms. He gave her a beseeching look.

"You're not a well man, my darling Jeb," she reminded him. "I won't be the cause behind your having a relapse and suffering a terrible decline. I've been too afraid of your dying these past weeks to bear the idea of losing you now. You must have your rest; you're not a well man yet."

Jeb nodded.

"I'll stop in to see you tonight," Amity said, "before I retire for the evening. I'll bring Grandpapa Witherspoon's Bible and read to you from the Good Book, as I did last night when Mammy, Serena, Denizia, and Big Tom joined us."

Again Jebediah nodded. From his pleased smile, Amity knew how much the Bible meant to him, and how overjoyed he was that she shared his love and respect for it.

Jeb, who had been awake quite a while, got comfortable on the daybed by the stove that Amity had just fired up. Amity noticed his eyes grow heavy. She'd scarcely left the room to go about her chores than he was fast asleep. She tiptoed back, kissed her fingertip, and pressed it against his mute lips.

"Until tonight," she promised.

After a quiet meal, as substantial as their plain fare allowed, the servants brought order to the kitchen and Amity attended to some needlework. When they had all finished their labors, they clustered around the potbellied stove, and Amity sat down on the settee beside Jeb and opened up Grandpapa Witherspoon's Bible.

In a melodious voice she began to read from the Psalms, squinting by the flickering candlelight to make out the words that at times were shadowy upon the printed page.

Occasionally one of the slaves would murmur, "Amen!" or "Praise His sweet name!" or "Halleluia!" when they heard a favorite passage.

Finally Amity's voice grew a bit husky from reading. Big Tom was openly yawning, and Denizia and Serena were swallowing their yawns. As for Mammy, her heavily jowled face had dropped forward to her ample chest, and she was softly snoring, lulled by the poetic phrases of the Old Testament.

Gently Amity closed the book.

"That's all for tonight," she said, yawning herself.

"I be goin' to bed then, Miss Amity, iffen there ain't nothing mo' yo' needin' me to be doin'."

"Good night, Denizia. Sleep well."

Big Tom stood up, stretching and yawning.

"I's plumb tuckered out. I be retirin' fo' de night, too, so's I can git up an' face all de work 'round here when comes de dawn."

"Sleep well, Big Tom. We can hope for a sunny and warm day tomorrow."

"Indeedy we can!" he said, and ambled off, a cheerful smile on his face.

Mammy and Serena said their good nights as well.

"Is there anything you would like before I retire for the evening?" Amity inquired of Jeb.

He looked at her, his eyes brimming, and she felt

a ripple of pleasure go through her as his adoring eyes expressed that there was one thing he wanted above all others—her!

With trembling hands she gave him the slate and a piece of rock that Big Tom had found down by the creek bed, which worked quite well in lieu of chalk.

A moment later Amity read the words on the slate, as Jeb suggested that she fix them a spot of tea before she departed for the evening.

"That sounds good," she admitted. She crossed to the water bucket, filled the pot, and set it on the potbellied stove. Then Amity replenished the fire with a few chunks of firewood that Big Tom had ricked in the corner wood box and slapped the dust and grit from her hands.

Jeb wordlessly patted the settee beside him. Feeling tense and nervous now that they were alone, Amity seated herself stiffly beside Jeb. Daring to be bold, he draped his arm around the back of the sofa.

As Amity relaxed, Jeb stroked her soft cheek with his forefinger. The movement lulled Amity, and before she realized it, her head was pillowed on his rugged shoulder. She felt total contentment.

Jeb shifted, reaching for the Bible that Amity had set aside. He moved it onto his lap, his fingers fanning through the pages. His fingers slowed, then carefully lifted individual pages.

He positioned the book solidly on his lap when it

opened to The Song of Songs. With a gentle touch, he roused Amity. Her tired eyes flickered open.

Jeb reached for his slate. He wrote, "Please read this for me." Then he took the chalk-stone, scratched out *me* and wrote *us* in its place.

"The Song of Songs?" Amity inquired.

Jeb nodded.

"Very well," she agreed.

Amity had not yet read The Song of Songs, for she had concentrated on reading from the New Testament, Proverbs, and Psalms.

Serena had told her that there were great love stories in the Bible, and Amity had read the story of Ruth. The Song of Songs was an undiscovered treasure, and as she read the precious words, she felt a sense of correctness that she should discover that book while snuggled in the arms of the man she loved.

As she read the words and occasionally looked up to find Jeb's eyes on her, a lump formed in Amity's throat. She realized Jeb had requested that she read from that book because the various songs of Solomon expressed so beautifully the feelings that Jeb had for her. His tongue could not tell her how he felt, and they hadn't the paper, quills, and ink sufficient for him to write to her.

Amity's voice grew tired, although the book was short, but she continued reading until she had finished the Song of Songs. For a moment the Bible rested open in her lap. Then Jeb shifted, removed his arm from around her, and carefully set the Bible on a nearby shelf. He reached for her again.

His cheek was close to hers, and she had only to move her head a fraction of an inch for their lips to meet, at first hesitantly, then with a precious hunger. Jeb rained kisses on her face.

"Oh, Amity. I've waited so long," he whispered. "I've dreamed of you every night. It's a miracle to have you in my arms. I love you Amity—I love you! And it's like sweet pain in my chest to realize that you love me, too."

"Oh Jeb, it may be shameless of me to admit it, but I do. I do!"

So accustomed had Amity become to the dialogue in dreadful penny romance novels and so caught up was she in the romance of the moment that she didn't realize at first that Jeb had spoken.

But Amity knew full well that Jeb *had* spoken, and in escalating horror she realized that it could not be a dream. In her dreams her Rebel had spoken in a soft, melodious drawl, the tones rippling and rich, sweet as pralines. Never had he uttered adoring words in the flat, clipped tongue of a Yankee!

"I adore you, Amity," Jeb whispered. "I've wanted you since that first night on the veranda in Atlanta when I was with Will. We'd noticed each other at the hospital, but we hadn't a chance to become introduced. I'd believed that I'd never see you again, but then Will invited me to accompany him to go calling on some belles and there you were. It was like a miracle. A gift from God. How I ached to talk to you, to court you."

Amity twisted out of his arms, shocked, dazed.

"Let go of me!" she cried, her voice shrill.

She struggled up from the settee. Startled Jeb let her go, releasing her before in her thrashing she burn herself against the potbellied stove.

Amity was flooded with confusion. Not knowing what to think, she was helpless to speak. She stared at Jeb as she gasped for breath. Her neatly ordered world was shattered, lying in jagged shards at her feet.

Their eyes met. Amity sensed that Jeb was as unsettled as she.

"I love you, Amity," he whispered in a voice that was no longer as shocking as when she'd first heard it. "And I will love you even if you vow to hate me with your dying breath because I am a Yankee."

Then Jeb began to tell her how much he had come to adore her, and why.

"We can't help it that I'm a Yankee while you're a Rebel born and bred. The War brought us together, Amity. Don't let politics drive us apart when there are so many things that so perfectly join us."

Jeb opened his arms to her, and she found herself moving into his hug like a sleepwalker. His lips—lips that could speak—sought hers. Helplessly, she responded to his tender ministrations. And she discovered herself even more thrilled by his loving attentions. Jeb—a sworn enemy—had become her beloved Yankee.

"I want you to marry me, Amity, and go North. I came South in search of my brother a year after I finished my own duty to the Union. Teddy lied about his age and enlisted to go fight Johnny Reb. I promised my mother I would find him and bring him back. But I arrived too late. I learned that he was killed at Shiloh.

"I prepared to return home with the sad news, but I was wounded near Dalton, knocked unconscious. Because I was a Yankee in civilian clothes, I was mistaken for a Rebel in homespun and put on the train of wounded bound for Atlanta. Enemies were everywhere, but they became people I liked." He cupped her face in his hands.

"And one of them I especially love. You!" He gave her lips a quick kiss and smiled.

"So you were forced to play the part of a mute?" Amity said, awed by what an act of will that had required.

"Yes. But the fact remains that I love you. I want you to be mine forever. Marry me, Amity, I beg of you."

"Jeb, this is so unexpected, so startling, that I don't know what to think. I don't know what to say. Go North? But—"

"My parents would adore you," he urged. "We have property and substantial holdings. You would never lack for anything, my beloved."

"Oh Jeb," Amity wailed, her words a tortured groan as she considered what it would mean to leave the land of her birth and rearing, maybe never to return. "You don't know what you're asking. I. . .I can't give you an answer. At least not right now. There's so much to think of—so many others to consider."

"Then say nothing for tonight, my darling. Give me your answer when comes the dawn."

"Very well," Amity agreed.

"I wish I could give you longer, my darling, but I must begin the long trek home soon. I will pray on your behalf, and if you pray for God's guidance, He will not forsake you. Come the dawn, you'll know your answer. We both will."

"Whatever happens, Jeb," Amity said, and her words squeaked as sudden tears salted her eyes and lips. "Know that I love you—and I always will."

"Then pray to God that it is His will that we be together, with everything settled in your heart as it already is in mine."

"I shall fall asleep tonight with that prayer on my lips."

"Before you do, I want to seal those honeyed lips with my kiss."

With the strength of Jeb's arms around her, his tall, rugged form shielding her, and his lips gentle and possessive on hers, Amity could have stayed in his embrace forever. She didn't know how she would ever find the strength to turn away if, after she prayed for guidance, the answer God gave her was not the one of her choosing.

Jeb released her, and Amity turned to depart, but then, unable to restrain himself, he drew her back into his arms for one last kiss.

Amity was about to shamelessly seek a third kiss—and a fourth—from him, but at that moment the teakettle began to whistle, preparing to issue a full-fledged scream. Hastily, Amity extricated herself from Jeb's arms and snatched the kettle from the stove before it could send Denizia and Mammy running to the kitchen.

If she chose to follow Jeb and in her own manner live out the story of Ruth, Amity realized that her loving servants would know soon enough the matters of the heart and the loving choices made.

thirteen

Amity awakened before dawn. For a moment she stared at the cover of her four poster canopy bed, organizing her thoughts and making plans for the day. But then she came fully awake and remembered the thrilling interlude with Jeb the night before.

Her heart ached with happiness, and she felt a ripple of joy as she realized that Jeb wanted her as his wife as much as she desired to spend the rest of her days with him. Amity Sheffield knew she would be content to love Jeb as they walked through life together trusting the Lord to guide them.

With a sense of eagerness, Amity arose and prepared to dress for the day. But as she smoothed her hair and heard Mammy coming up the staircase to lay out her clothing and help her into her dress, she paused to consider what the future would demand that she leave behind—perhaps forever—if the North and South never reconciled their differences.

In moving North, she might be viewed as a Southern Rebel for the rest of her days, and the South's citizenry, knowing she had chosen to link herself to a Yankee, would view her as a betrayer.

Amity thought of her papa, an older man who had galloped off to war, ready to fight and die for the Confederate nation that had spawned him. He couldn't have believed in all of the C.S.A.'s tenets, but tradition and loyalty had guided him to do his part to preserve a way of life he had always known.

Amity stared at her troubled eyes reflected in the beveled looking glass in the marble-topped vanity, and she realized that she was as fearful as she was eager, as hesitant as she was optimistic.

"Change is frightening," she whispered to herself, then tried to rub away the quick sprinkle of goose bumps that rose on her skin. It was human nature, she realized, to cling to the familiar rather than reach out for the fearful unknown, even when the future promised happiness.

There were no guarantees. Jeb loved her, of that she was sure. But was it enough? Could she leave behind her father and others she held dear to follow Jeb anywhere he might choose to go?

Mammy arrived and began the process of lacing Amity's stays. From what the servant didn't say, Amity knew that, as usual, nothing had gone unnoticed by her. Mammy had tried to tell her that Jeb could talk, but Amity had been adamant in her refusal to hear what her Mammy had been telling her.

Had Mammy been listening from her doorway as Jeb offered his proposal of marriage? Amity couldn't help smiling as she suspected that it was probably so.

She gave a heavy sigh as she considered the conflicts that faced her, and her mind swirled with possible ramifications. Either choice she made had drawbacks, just as both possibilities offered benefits.

The tender hand Mammy laid on Amity's shoulder conveyed to her that Mammy knew and understood.

"I be goin' an' wakin' up Mist' Jeb," Mammy said.

"Let him sleep," Amity murmured. "He needs his rest. I'll take a breakfast tray to him later."

"Yes, Miss Amity. Whatever yo' say." Mammy crossed to open the drapes. "My, but it's a pretty day. A bit overcast, but—"

"It's dawned the most beautiful day of my life," Amity murmured, "and would be still if it were pouring down rain."

She bit back more words, not yet wanting to tell Mammy that Jeb was a Yankee, and that he'd sought her hand.

"And it might rain. Oh my! Lord have mercy!" Mammy gasped.

"What is it?" Amity asked, shaken when she heard the fright in Mammy's voice.

She rushed to her side. From their second-story vantage point they could see a procession moving toward their mansion. Amity recognized Cousin Philomen's wagon and mule, Mister Raynor's saddle mule, and Miss Ophelia dressed in black, seated grimly at Philomen's side, surrounded by a motley assortment of sharecroppers and impoverished planters. No doubt these men were veterans of the War for Separation and carried physical scars, weaknesses, and painful imperfections that served as reminders of what the battle had cost them.

"What on earth?"

"Quick, Miss Amity, yo' run down t' meet 'em, and stall 'em as best yo' can—"

"But—"

"Do as yo' tol', Lambie. Dem folks's up to no good. Believe me, yo' ol' Mammy be knowin' a lynch mob when she sees one! Dey's after yo' Yankee man."

Amity felt faint.

"No!" she cried.

"Yo' keep yo' head an' wits about you, an' go down there, Miss Amity," Mammy ordered, giving her a gentle shove toward the door. "An' you act like they ain't no accursed Yankee never been nowheres near this house. An' you play the part as if Mist' Jeb's life depended on it—because it does!"

"What are you going to do, Mammy?" Amity cried, realizing that she'd always trusted in Mammy's wise counsel. The aged black woman had an ability to miraculously make bad situations acceptable through the sheer power and stoicism of her personality. Mammy had unbending ethics and a well-developed sense of what was right and what was wrong.

"Don't ask, child. Yo' be better off if yo' don't know nothin' about what yo' mammy's goin' to do."

Amity threw a wrap around her suddenly icy body and ventured from Grandpapa Witherspoon's mansion to greet her half-sister and the grim-faced lynch mob.

The welcoming words that Amity had selected flew from her mind when she saw the savage sneer on Ophelia's hate-filled face, noticed her red-rimmed eyes, and realized that the dark clothing signified that her half sister was consigned to the wearing of widow's weeds.

"You hussy! You tawdry harlot!" Ophelia cried her rage. "Where is he? Where's the vile Yankee blue-belly you've been sheltering, while his kind have allowed my husband to die in a wretched northern prison and caused our papa to succumb in a hospital after growing septic from his wounds?"

Amity felt the news about Papa and Schuyler's deaths like a hammer blow, but then her thoughts flew to the needs of the living and the man she loved.

"There's no Yankee here," Amity said. She didn't believe she lied, for in her mind people were no longer Northerner or Southerner, Union or Confederate, Yankee or Rebel. They were all human beings created by God. She and Jeb were in a special family—Christians—united with other believers. In this world they would never know some of their brothers and sisters in Christ, but in the hereafter they would recognize strangers as dear siblings in faith.

The sisters stood eye to eye, toe to toe. Without any warning, Ophelia slapped Amity with such a force that a crimson stain spread across the younger woman's pale cheek.

Amity bore the insult and the pain without reaction, but Mammy charged forward, the fire of indignation in her eyes.

"How's come yo' striking my baby?" Mammy angrily demanded as she came thundering down the front veranda steps, impervious to the cold.

"What's goin' on here?" Her black face was set in a forbidding glower as her hot gaze swept to take in the rag-tag group of Southerners gathered around her.

"We're looking to take custody of the Yankee y'all been harborin' here, Mammy," Mister Raynor spoke up. "Y'all best be handing him over."

There was a rope coiled on the horn of the saddle in which he shifted as he waited. Nearby stood a tall tree.

"They ain't no Yankee gemp'mum here, Mist' Raynor, sir."

"Ain't no *gentleman* to be found in the entire North," Cousin Philomen spat in a bitter tone.

"Don't try to tell us that he's not here," Ophelia cried in a strident voice. "We know better. The doctor you called has been telling the countryside about the Yankee he treated at Amity Sheffield's request."

"That gemp'mum never spoke a word to me, Miss Ophelia," Mammy said. "An' I tended dat sickly man day an' night 'til he was well enough to leave."

"I don't believe you," Ophelia murmured. "Nor do the men who are accompanying me." She swiveled to face them.

"You all have my permission to search my grandpapa's house. Leave not a nook nor a cranny unsearched."

She turned back to Mammy and Amity with a triumphant glint in her tear-ravaged, hate-filled eyes.

"Y'all go right ahead," Mammy invited graciously, while Amity quailed within. "Yo' won't find no Yankee. Yo' won't find nothing but de late Mist' Buford's household help an' the late Mist' Morgan Sheffield's servants in the care o' Miss Amity here, who inherited us from her late mama."

"Gentlemen," Miss Ophelia said, "make yourselves at home. Search as long and as thoroughly as you like."

"This isn't your home. It's mine," Amity flared.

"This plantation is bequeathed to me. Grandpapa Witherspoon was no kin to you. But rather than thwart you, Ophelia, I will agree," Amity added after a special look had passed between her and Mammy. "We have nothing to hide. So, gentlemen, as the mistress of this manor, I bid you welcome and invite you to search. I'll have my servants prepare a repast so that you can refresh yourselves before you begin your long ride home."

Ophelia, realizing she was no longer in control, gave her young half-sister a murderous look. Rather than enter the home that was Amity's rightful domain, the older woman stood outside, shivering beneath a tree. She wept with rage, disappointment, and frustration at what she was unable to control and manipulate.

Although the search took less than an hour, to Amity it seemed to last an eternity. At any moment she expected to hear brawl-like sounds of victory as the men located Jeb where Mammy had secreted him.

But in her heart, she believed that her sister and the lynch mob would leave without satisfaction, for she knew what the Good Book said about protection. If the posse was successful in locating Jeb, it would be only because the Lord had allowed it.

Finally the mob left after enjoying the tarts that Serena had prepared. It was apparent that everyone except Miss Ophelia was feeling more convivial as they rode away.

For long minutes Amity stared after them, stunned, tears running down her face when she looked out over the meadows. She felt such relief that the blood-lusting mob had not laid a hand on Jebediah.

He seemed gone, truly gone, and Mammy had said nary a word about it, suspecting that the posse would circle back to check again a short while later. She wished to continue to protect Amity from knowledge that the group of men might try to wrest from her.

Two hours passed. Amity's grief deepened when she realized that she would never see Jeb again. While she had stalled the mob at the front of the house, Mammy and Serena must have sent Big Tom out the back way, supporting the weakened Yankee until he was protected by the woods. Big Tom would then have rushed back to the house so that his absence would not arouse suspicions. No doubt Jeb was weakly making his way through the woods, cold and without food, not knowing where he'd find shelter for the night.

"Whyfore yo' cryin', Miss Amity? They's gone. An' while they might be back, I don't think it's going to be today, and by—"

"I'm crying because I miss him, Mammy, and because I love him. Jeb wanted me to marry him. He wanted for us to go North. He said he'd await my answer until morning. But now he's gone before I could give it to him."

"And what might you've decided to tell Mist' Jeb?"

"Yes, Mammy. My answer was going to be yes!"

"Then tell him, Lambie. He's here. I know this ol' house like the back of my hand. I 'spects I's the only one left that knows dey's a little hidden closet in the attic, there from the day's when Mist' Buford's papa planned de home. We had jus' enough time to get Mist' Jeb and all his belongings into it before the lynchers was ready to search de house."

At that moment Jeb stepped outside and laid his hand on Amity's shaking shoulder.

"It's not too late for me to accept your answer, Amity. But now I know that I must leave this home, even as I realize that I can't—won't—go alone. I want to take you with me. I want to take all of you home with me."

"Do you mean it, Jeb?" Amity asked, realizing that she could never be happy without Mammy and Serena, and that fond as she was of Denizia and Big Tom, and they of her, they wouldn't want to abandon the plantation that had been their lifelong home.

Things in the Southland were changing. Grandpapa Witherspoon's plantation was now hers, to do with as she would. Jeb had told her that his family possessed wealth, that she would never want for material things. That meant she could give Denizia and Big Tom not only their freedom, but the deed to the plantation as well.

Serena, Amity believed, would want to go North to the land of opportunity where she could earn her livelihood with her skills and intelligence. And as for Mammy, Amity needed her to go with them, wanted her to go. Mammy had been more of a mother to her than the woman who had given birth to her.

Mammy had always been there, and Mammy would want to always be there, to be the loving grandmother to Amity's own children. She would help Amity and Jeb guide their children in the ways of the Lord.

"I'm afraid we may have to walk all the way to Atlanta," Jeb apologized. "But once we encounter Yankee forces, there should be no problems for us."

Amity laughed.

"For years I've feared the Yankees. Now I long for the sight of them," she drawled.

"And I'm afraid that while I have money in the North, my sweet, I'm an impoverished man in the Confederacy."

"I have an inheritance, Jeb, to stake us on our freedom journey. It's from Rosalynn, a one-time Boston debutante who would understand and approve of us using her money in this way."

Amity smiled as an autumn shower began to drizzle on the veranda roof with the slow, lazy passion of a storm that would soon find itself spent.

Mammy sighed with satisfaction and shuffled into the house, murmuring to herself about the packing at hand, the tasks to attend to, and the heirlooms that should be collected to be passed on to Miss Amity's young.

"Take what you want," Jeb encouraged her. "But I can promise you, Miss Amity's children and mine will have everything they need: a mother, a father—"

"And Mammy," Amity assured.

"An' de Lord!"

A Letter To Our Readers

Dear Reader:

In order that we might better contribute to your reading enjoyment, we would appreciate your taking a few minutes to respond to the following questions. When completed, please return to the following:

Karen Carroll, Editor
Heartsong Presents
P.O. Box 719
Uhrichsville, Ohio 44683

1. Did you enjoy reading *When Comes the Dawn*?
    ☐ Very much. I would like to see more books by this author!
    ☐ Moderately
       I would have enjoyed it more if _____

    _____

2. Are you a member of *Heartsong Presents*? Yes   No
    If no, where did you purchase this book? _____

    _____

3. What influenced your decision to purchase this book? (Circle those that apply.)

    Cover   Back cover copy

    Title   Friends

    Publicity   Other _____

4. On a scale from 1 (poor) to 10 (superior), please rate the following elements.

    ___Heroine   ___Plot

    ___Hero   ___Inspirational theme

    ___Setting   ___Secondary characters

5. What settings would you like to see covered in *Heartsong Presents* books?

  _____

  _____

6. What are some inspirational themes you would like to see treated in future books?_____

  _____

  _____

7. Would you be interested in reading other *Heartsong Presents* titles?   Yes   No

8. Please circle your age range:

Under 18	18-24	25-34
35-45	46-55	Over 55

9. How many hours per week do you read? _____

Name _____

Occupation _____

Address _____

City _____ State _____ Zip _____

HEARTS♥NG PRESENTS books are inspirational romances in contemporary and historical settings, designed to give you an enjoyable, spirit-lifting reading experience.

add a little MYSTERY to your romance!

TWO GREAT INSPIRATIONAL ROMANCES WITH JUST A TOUCH OF MYSTERY
BY MARLENE J. CHASE

_____*The Other Side of Silence*—Anna Durham finds a purpose for living in the eyes of a needy child and a reason to love in the eyes of a lonely physician...but first the silence of secrets must be broken. HP6 BHSB-07 $2.95.

_____*This Trembling Cup*—A respite on a plush Wisconsin resort may just be the thing for Angie Carlson's burn-out—or just the beginning of a devious plot unraveling and the promise of love. HP5 BHSB-05 $2.95.

Inspirational Romance at its Best from one of America's Favorite Authors!

FOUR HISTORICAL ROMANCES
BY COLLEEN L. REECE

___ *A Torch for Trinity*—When Trinity Mason sacrifices her teaching ambitions for a one-room school, her life— and Will Thatcher's—will never be the same. HP1 BHSB-01 $2.95

___*Candleshine*-A sequel to *A Torch for Trinity*—With the onslaught of World War II, Candleshine Thatcher dedicates her life to nursing, and then her heart to a brave Marine lieutenant. HP7 BHSB-06 $2.95

___*Wildflower Harvest*—Ivy Ann and Laurel were often mistaken for each other...was it too late to tell one man the truth? HP2 BHSB-02 $2.95

___ *Desert Rose*-A sequel to *Wildflower Harvest*—When Rose Birchfield falls in love with one of Michael's letters, and then with a cowboy named Mike, no one is more confused than Rose herself. HP8 BHSB-08 $2.95